LONG SHADOWS

When Fiona Dalrymple's grandmother dies, Fiona is shocked to learn that Doreen wasn't actually her grandmother at all ... Her grandfather's first wife, Ellie Marsden, is still alive and when Fiona meets her, Ellie has a further shock for her: she also has a brother. What's more, Tim has disappeared and Fiona is charged with the task of finding him ... so why does Rory, Tim's handsome boss, seem intent on being more of a hindrance than a help?

MARGARET MOUNSDON

LONG SHADOWS

Complete and Unabridged

LINFORD
Leicester

First published in Great Britain in 2009

First Linford Edition
published 2010

British Library CIP Data

Mounsdon, Margaret.
    Long shadows. - -
    (Linford romance library)
    1. Family secrets- -Fiction.
    2. Missing persons- -Investigation- -Fiction.
    3. Romantic suspense novels.
    4. Large type books.
    I. Title II. Series
    823.9'2–dc22

    ISBN 978–1–44480–225–2

Published by
F. A. Thorpe (Publishing)
Anstey, Leicestershire

Set by Words & Graphics Ltd.
Anstey, Leicestershire
Printed and bound in Great Britain by
T. J. International Ltd., Padstow, Cornwall

This book is printed on acid-free paper

1

Fiona frowned and re-read the letter. The heat of the day had to be going to her head. The letter in her hand was signed Ellie Marsden and Ellie Marsden appeared to be her grandmother.

I was so sorry to read of your sad loss, Fiona read as she tried to make sense of the words on the piece of paper in front of her.

It's been many years since Doreen and I met. I always meant to get in touch but my husband's business interests were worldwide and we were rarely in one place for long. I shouldn't have let things slide and I would dearly like to make amends. I have so much to tell you and now that my husband is retired we have settled back in England. Perhaps you would like to come to tea some time soon, shall we say on Thursday? I look forward to seeing you.

Fiona put down the letter and, opening the kitchen door, walked out into the garden. She picked up a watering can and filling it, began to water her tomato plants. They were wilting in the July sun and their furled leaves looked how Fiona felt — completely robbed of all the love she had always thought she had.

Ever since the loss of her beloved grandmother three weeks ago, she had been in a daze. Her death had left Fiona bereft and, so she had thought, alone in the world. Now it seemed Doreen Weir wasn't even her real grandmother. This Ellie Marsden was.

Fiona refilled her can and turned her attention to the runner beans. Watering her vegetables helped her think in times of stress. She had lived with her grandparents since she was a baby. Rose Cottage was the only home she had ever known, and it had been filled with warmth and love. Her grandfather had been a wonderful man and despite his age had more than a twinkle in his eye.

'Hello.' A voice disturbed Fiona's thoughts and she looked up. 'I've made some strawberry shortcake.' Mrs Shaw poked her head over the hawthorn hedge. 'Thought you might fancy a piece, seeing as it's made from your own home grown strawberries.'

Fiona put down her watering can with a sigh. Mrs Shaw was her neighbour and she was nosy. There was nothing that went on at Rose Cottage without her knowing about it, but for all her nosiness she had a kind heart. Fiona realised her salad lunch had been a long time ago and some strawberry shortcake would make an excellent snack.

'Come round for a cup of tea,' Fiona felt duty bound to offer.

'Be with you in a jiffy.' Mrs Shaw beamed at her then disappeared from view.

'My, it's a hot day.' Mrs Shaw settled down under Fiona's sunshade and placed two generous slabs of strawberry shortcake onto two willow-patterned plates. 'Earl Grey.' She watched Fiona pour out two cups of tea. 'Bergamot, just what I need to pick me up.'

Fiona bit into a piece of shortcake. It crumbled in her mouth. Mrs Shaw was an excellent cook.

'Pity we haven't got any cream to go with it,' Mrs Shaw attacked her own slice with a fork, 'it would go down a treat.'

'I shouldn't really be eating this,' Fiona admitted, trying not to calorie count.

'Nonsense.' Mrs Shaw looked affronted. 'You don't need to lose weight, besides a tall girl like you can carry a few extra pounds and you've lost quite a bit of weight recently I'd say.'

Fiona smiled. Mrs Shaw didn't hold with diets and Fiona had to admit her shortcake was delicious.

'Are you going to take a little holiday?' Mrs Shaw paused delicately. 'Now things are settled? If you want to go away I can always keep an eye on the cottage for you and water your plants. A change of scenery would do you good.'

Fiona shook her head. 'I don't think so.'

'Your grandmother wouldn't have wanted you to mope, you know,' Mrs Shaw pointed out gently.

'I know. Perhaps I'll take a few days off later in the month.'

'That's the idea. Doesn't do to be on your own. When I think of that George Ross,' Mrs Shaw's sunny smile slipped, 'he should have been here with you.'

Fiona winced. It still hurt to think about her ex-fiancé. She had thought George was the love of her life and had been devastated when, two months before the wedding, he had suggested a cooling-off period. She had been even more devastated when, six weeks later, he had married the girl who had been going to style Fiona's hair for the wedding!

'Let's not talk about George,' Fiona said trying to make light of the matter. Once Mrs Shaw got on her high horse there was no stopping her and she'd said, all there was to say about George Ross — several times.

'Actually,' Fiona hesitated, remembering her letter. She would have to be careful how much she told Mrs Shaw, but with her knowledge of local affairs, she might be the one person who would know about Ellie Marsden. 'Does the name Ellie Marsden mean anything to you?'

Mrs Shaw spluttered on her shortbread and, putting down her cup of tea, dabbed delicately at her lips. 'Crumb went down the wrong way,' she coughed.

'Ellie Marsden?' Fiona repeated when Mrs Shaw had recovered herself. 'Have you heard of her?'

'Why do you ask?' Mrs Shaw toyed with her fork then pushed half her shortbread away uneaten.

Fiona's interest quickened. Mrs Shaw was not naturally discreet and Fiona had known instantly from the expression on her face that the name was not unknown to her.

'Because the funeral directors forwarded me a condolence letter from her.'

'I see,' Mrs Shaw spoke slowly.

Fiona folded her hands and waited patiently. Mrs Shaw seemed to be having trouble choosing her words.

'Did your grandmother never mention her to you?'

Fiona shook her head. 'Was she some sort of business contact of my grandfather's, do you know?'

In his professional life Angus Weir had had several female partners. Fiona had met several of them, but she didn't recall an Ellie Marsden.

Her grandparents' marriage had been a volatile one, caused mainly by her grandfather's frequent absences from home on business. Angus Weir was a handsome, charismatic man and a successful lawyer. He also had an eye for the ladies. On more than one occasion Fiona's grandmother had had to intercept personal calls to the cottage from grateful female clients who had been seeking to further their relationship.

'No, she wasn't exactly a business contact,' Mrs Shaw said slowly.

'You know her then?'

'I met her once.'

'Can you tell me anything about her?' Fiona asked.

Mrs Shaw looked at her watch. 'I really should be going. Jim will be wanting his tea. Likes it on the dot of six he does, especially on bowls night.'

'But you haven't finished your Earl Grey yet Mrs Shaw,' Fiona pointed out, 'and you've hardly even touched your shortbread — and it's delicious.'

Mrs Shaw picked up her cup then put it down again without drinking any of the contents. Her face was screwed up in anguish.

'Ellie Marsden?' Fiona prompted

again, wondering why Mrs Shaw was looking so agitated.

'It really is none of my business, Fiona,' Mrs Shaw said, 'and if your grandmother had wanted you to know about her then I'm sure she would have told you herself.'

Fiona bit down her frustration. Pulling hen's teeth would appear to be easier than getting information about this wretched Ellie Marsden from Mrs Shaw.

'She says she's my grandmother.'

A look of relief appeared on Mrs Shaw's face. 'You know? I didn't realise. I promised Doreen I would never breathe a word about her and I never have.'

'I don't think it would be breaking your promise to my grandmother, now,' Fiona amended, 'and I do need to know something about Ellie Marsden if I'm going to meet up with her.'

'You are? When?'

'She suggested a date next week.'

'I see.' Mrs Shaw plaited her fingers,

all the while biting her lower lip. Eventually she appeared to come to a decision. She nodded. 'Ellie Marsden was your grandfather's first wife.'

Fiona managed to hide her surprise. Now she'd got Mrs Shaw talking, she didn't want to spook her into silence by interrupting.

'The marriage didn't last long. I don't know the details but the first time I saw you, you were a babe in arms — Ellie Marsden's arms. I'd called round for a bowl of sugar.' Mrs Shaw tossed back her head as if daring Fiona to challenge. They both knew the bowl of sugar would be a pretext to find out what was going on next door, but Fiona was prepared on this occasion to let it ride. 'That was the only time I saw Ellie Marsden. She was seated on the sofa, and you were asleep in her arms. That's it really.' Mrs Shaw lapsed into silence.

'I see.'

There was a lot more she would have liked to ask Mrs Shaw but Fiona sensed she'd had all the information she was going to get.

'Was there nothing about her in Doreen's private papers?' Mrs Shaw asked.

'I haven't gone through them all.'

Fiona thought of the crammed suitcase in the spare bedroom. Her grandmother had not thrown out anything, from Fiona's first drawing, to her school certificates. So far she hadn't plucked up the courage to sort through the mountain of paperwork.

'Perhaps you'd better.' Mrs Shaw patted her arm. 'Now, I must be on my way. Thank you for the tea and don't forget, I'm only next door if you need me.'

Fiona watched her neighbour take the short cut through the hedge back to her own cottage.

For all her faults Mrs Shaw had been a tower of strength over the past six months and Fiona didn't think she would have been able to manage without her. Nothing had been too much trouble and Fiona would be forever in her debt.

Although it was early evening, the heat of the sun hadn't abated and the flagstones on the patio were still hot under Fiona's sandaled feet. She crammed her ancient sun hat onto her head and picked up her discarded watering can. After the beans there were the roses to attend to and then the bed of mint needed weeding.

It was twilight before Fiona eventually went back indoors. Her fingernails were dirt-engrained and her t-shirt would have to be binned, but the garden was feeling better and so was Fiona.

After she washed her hands her eyes fell on the discarded letter on the kitchen table. She picked it up, read it again, then crossed to the telephone and began to dial the number at the top of the page.

2

Fiona was surprised to learn that Ellie and her husband Frank lived less than ten miles away from her village of Grange Heath, but their detached executive property on an exclusive estate was as about as far removed from Rose Cottage as it was possible to be.

Impressive iron gates guarded the private access to the residential estate bordering the golf course and Fiona's credentials were double-checked by private security personnel before she was allowed to drive through into the compound. An ornamental fountain graced the entrance and Fiona found herself wishing she'd washed the dust off her ancient hatchback before starting out.

Gleaming high performance cars graced the driveways and they were all parked neatly in designated bays.

The postage stamp squares of lawn in front of each property were mown to within an inch of their lives and Fiona thought lovingly of her own daisy-strewn patch of lawn that badly needed a mow. No daisy or buttercup would dare show itself here. With places like this she thought, it was no wonder wildlife was fighting for survival.

Ignoring the butterflies dancing crazily in her stomach and following Ellie's careful instructions, Fiona drove around the crescent shaped drive until she found April Cottage. Her lips twitched in amusement again. If this was a cottage, then her little dwelling was a rabbit hutch. There was an impressive double garage, leaded light windows that bore testament to a window cleaner's diligence and artfully displayed tubs of geraniums on the doorstep — all added to the general effect of affluence.

Now she was here, Fiona was hit by a sense of panic. This wasn't her sort of place and she just knew that the residents wouldn't be her kind of

14

people at all. She worked in the local library and what little spare time she had was spent in her beloved garden or enjoying the occasional night out with her girlfriends.

These people were high-powered professionals who had second homes in Spain and spent their winters ski-ing or in the Caribbean.

Controlling her racing nerves with several deep breaths Fiona turned off her car engine. Before she could even remove the key from the ignition, the front door to April Cottage was yanked open.

A tall, well groomed woman dressed in a light cashmere jumper and plain blue skirt stood in the doorway. Fiona gulped at the sight of her. The July day, although not as hot as last week, was still warm and she had dressed for comfort in faded cotton t-shirt, floaty skirt and sandals. Ellie, if this was Ellie Marsden and not some paid flunky, was wearing tights and court shoes. A string of pearls graced her neck and she didn't have a hair out of place.

Fiona flicked back her mane of dark hair. She knew it badly needed a cut but ever since George's elopement with the village hairdresser Fiona had foregone her six weekly trim and, apart from snipping at her fringe every now and then, her hair hadn't been near a pair of scissors for months. Now she was wishing she had paid a tad more attention to her personal grooming. She looked down at her hands. At least she had managed to dig the earth out from under her fingernails.

'Fiona?' The smile on Ellie's face was hesitant as Fiona eased her long legs out of the hatchback. She reached over to the passenger seat for the bunch of garden flowers she'd made up last night.

'Hello, er — what should I call you?' Fiona straightened up, unprepared for the exuberance of Ellie's hug as she rushed down the drive to greet her, squashing the flowers to Fiona's chest as she did so.

'Come along in. I'm Ellie. Frank's out playing golf so we'll have the place to ourselves.' Ellie accepted the proffered bouquet. 'Dahlias, how lovely.'

'I grew them myself,' Fiona explained.

'I'll put them in water, then we'll go out on the terrace, shall we?'

Fiona saw, with a sinking heart, that Ellie already had a vase of fresh carnations on her hall table. Ellie caught her looking at them.

'Frank arranges for me to have a delivery every week, but you know what?' she added with her sweet smile, tweaking a purple petal as she spoke, 'These mean more to me than all the shop bought flowers in the world. Come along in.'

The hall smelt of lavender polish and every surface gleamed. Feeling most out of place, Fiona followed Ellie through to the sunny state-of-the-art kitchen. Not so much as a single biscuit crumb littered the pristine marble worktops and there was no smell of warm toast or reheated lunch leftovers

17

that formed the staple of Fiona's diet.

'There.' Ellie hastily arranged the flowers in a vase and put them on the kitchen sill. 'Now let me have a good look at you.'

The two women faced each other. Fiona felt hot and gauche under Ellie's cool gaze. She could see no resemblance to herself in the older woman's clear complexion and pale blue eyes. Fiona's skin was tanned from long hours working in her beloved garden and her eyes and hair were both a dark, velvety brown. How could this woman with her peaches and cream complexion and clear blue eyes be her grandmother?

'You are so like your mother,' she said gently, stroking Fiona's face. 'I'm sorry,' she removed her hand instantly as Fiona stiffened under her touch. 'That was thoughtless of me, invading your body space like that. I do apologise. Please, shall we go outside?'

Happy to be in the fresh air, Fiona took a few moments out to inspect the garden. Like the house, it was too perfect. There was no stray fallen blossom on the lawn, or heap of rotting compost piled up in a far corner behind an old shed that had seen better days. Ellie's shed was a neat little construction straight out of a fairy tale.

'Are you very angry with me?' Ellie asked as they sat down on a swing chair under a canopy.

'I'm sorry?' Fiona frowned, feeling she had missed something.

'I had no choice you see.'

'Er — could we start again?' Fiona asked. 'I'm not sure I'm getting all this.'

'Of course, how silly of me. I always talk too much when I'm nervous. Would you like to ask me some questions and I'll do my best to answer them?'

'I don't know where to start,' Fiona admitted.

'Well, I'll ask you a question.' Ellie leaned forward eagerly. 'Did Doreen ever mention me at all?'

Fiona shook her head. 'Neither did Grandfather.'

'Angus,' Ellie said the name with a slow smile. 'He truly was my first love. Sometimes I think I behaved foolishly walking out on him the way I did, but I was young and easily made jealous.'

'What happened between you?' Fiona asked.

'I over-reacted when I thought one of his female partners was getting too friendly. I took Gillian, your mother, with me and went back to my mother. She never really got on with Angus and she banned him from the house. The next thing I knew he had gone abroad to work and . . . ' She shrugged. 'It doesn't do to dwell on these things and it was all so long ago. I've been with my beloved Frank for over thirty years now and he's never given me a day's anguish.'

By the way Ellie was speaking about him, Fiona had the sneaking suspicion that, despite her thirty years with Frank, Angus was still the love of Ellie's life.

'And you never saw Angus again?'

'No. He had access to Gillian, of course, and she often stayed with him and Doreen, but I never did. Unfortunately Frank and I were never blessed with children.' Ellie smoothed down her skirt, picking at an imaginary stray piece of fluff with her fingers. 'That was what made you and . . . ' she hesitated, 'your mother, so special.'

Fiona was having difficulty keeping her opinions to herself. If she was so special, how come this woman had quite simply walked out of her life?

'Mrs Shaw said I was a babe in arms when you left me with Doreen.'

Ellie's fingers stalled. 'Mrs Shaw? Was she the next door neighbour?'

'She still is and she remembers you.'

Ellie looked as if she were badly in need of a stiff gin and tonic. 'I looked after you for six weeks after your parents' accident. Frank and I were on a trip home when it happened. He was working in Singapore at the time and only had a short leave of absence so he had to fly back without me. I was at my wits' end. I didn't know what to do. I couldn't take a young baby back to the Far East. We lived in a high rise flat and we didn't have the facilities to look after you. It broke my heart to leave you with Doreen but I had no choice. You weren't unhappy at Rose Cottage were you?'

'No,' Fiona conceded, 'I had the best childhood any child could have.'

'I'm so pleased.' Ellie put out a hand as if to stroke her arm but, changing her mind, began picking at her skirt again.

'Why did you never write to me or send me a birthday card,' Fiona demanded, 'if I meant so much to you?'

Ellie turned away from Fiona's searching gaze and looked down the garden. 'I intended to, but I was ill when I returned to Singapore, I think it was a delayed reaction to all the stress. Then Frank was transferred to China. When I recovered my health I wrote to you but I never received a reply. I'm not sure if my letters even got through. We were based in a remote province and communication with the outside world was difficult. We were there for five years.'

'Did you never come back to England?'

'Occasionally after our tour of duty ended in the Far East,' Ellie admitted.

'And you still didn't think to come and see me?'

'There was so much to do when we got back and . . . '

Fiona felt a surge of resentment building up inside her for this elegant woman. 'What you're saying is a child would have ruined your ex-pat lifestyle? You didn't want to be bothered with your only grandchild, so you chose to airbrush me out of your life altogether?'

The words danced in the air between them. Fiona hadn't meant to raise her voice, but she could see by the wounded expression on Ellie's face that her words had found their target.

'I think perhaps I'd better leave,'

Fiona said, 'before I say something I regret.'

'It wasn't like that at all.' Ellie's voice was a hollow whisper.

'No, I'm sure it wasn't.'

'You don't understand. We simply couldn't afford to bring up two children.'

'Two children?'

'Yes.'

'Didn't you say you and Frank didn't have any children of your own?'

'Yes.'

All around them the garden noises stilled and a pain in her chest reminded Fiona that she had forgotten to breathe.

'You're right. I don't understand.'

'You have an older brother. His name is Tim. I would have liked him to be here to meet you today,' Ellie moistened her lips with the tip of her tongue, 'only he's gone missing, you see.'

3

Rory Grainger strode through the reception area casting a quick professional eye over the desk and his staff. A full complement of receptionists was working the desk and all were wearing correct uniform.

'Hi, Rory,' one of the beauty therapists greeted him as she made her way to the fitness centre.

He returned her smile. Although he was on first name terms with all the staff, he liked also to maintain a sense of authority and while everyone respected him and knew they could enjoy a joke with him in the staff room over a cup of coffee, they were careful not to overstep the mark.

'All present and correct.' A receptionist showed him the registration book correctly made up and annotated with chalet numbers and times of arrival of the most recent guests.

Rory quickly scanned the entries then nodded approval. 'That all seems fine,' he said. 'Any problems?'

'No new ones,' she smiled back at him.

'That's the way I like it.'

One or two guests drifted through from the pool having taken an early morning dip before breakfast. Their towelling robes displayed the exclusive logo of The Hills, a discreetly mono-grammed TH in grey letters entwined on a luxurious cream background.

The lettering suited the discreet image the proprietors wished to por-tray, efficient and state of the art.

Guests were accommodated in detached chalets around the main building which had originally been a private house, built in the Victorian era by an industrialist. After the last of the family had died off, the property had been sold and con-verted to a luxury hotel and health hydro.

During their stay, visitors had com-plete use of all the facilities offered. They could enjoy a quiet stroll in the landscaped gardens followed by after-noon tea on the terrace or later take a drink in the bar and have dinner in one of several top quality restaurants.

Those on a more rigorous regime could work out in the leisure complex, which included an Olympic style swimming pool, a steam room and sauna and a fully equipped beauty salon.

Although The Hills catered for the occasional pampered media mogul or film star, most of their clientele were professional people who needed a quiet place to relax, unwind and de-stress from the hectic round of their daily lives. At The Hills they knew their every need would be catered for with the minimum of fuss.

'Has there been any news from Tim?' asked the head groundsman, dressed in off-duty open-necked shirt and clean jeans, as he strolled into the main house.

Rory's lips tightened. 'Nothing as yet.'

'He's been gone ten days now.'

'I realise that, Bill.' Rory was careful not to let any feeling show through as he spoke to the groundsman. Guests were very quick to pick up on the slightest tension amongst the staff. 'But the first week was official holiday, after all,' Rory reminded him.

'That's all very well,' Bill's expression of annoyance did not ease up, 'but I can't manage everything on my own.'

'No one is suggesting you should,' Rory explained patiently. 'I'll detail one of the maintenance men to help out while you're still a man short.'

'Mr Grainger,' a voice interrupted them.

Rory turned around instantly with a pleasant smile.

'Mrs Entwhistle?' He made it a policy to officially identify all guests by their name, even if they were fully booked with several dozen guests — as they were now. 'What can I do for you?'

'I know I stipulated orange juice for breakfast in my chalet after my swim but one of the therapists has recommended I try white tea.'

'It will be done,' he said. 'Leave it to me.'

She smiled up at him. 'I have to say, Mr Grainger, the attention to detail at The Hills is superb and last night's meal was a dream.'

'I'll be delighted to pass your compliments on to the chef,' he promised.

When he turned back to speak to Bill he had already gone. With a thoughtful frown Rory made his way to his office.

The pile of paperwork never seemed to reduce in size, he thought as he eyed up the mountain of memos in his in tray. What he really needed was an efficient personal assistant, but the last one had left with the swimming instructor when he had decided to return to Australia, and Rory had not had time to go through the process of recruiting a replacement.

Quickly checking his email inbox to see if there was anything new from Tim, he replied to a few enquiries for information and signed a couple of urgent orders for supplies for the physiotherapist.

The success of The Hills was a testament to Rory's superb professionalism. His own background could not possibly have been more different from that of the majority of his guests.

Born in Liverpool to a railway worker father and mother whose poor health had meant frequent stays in hospital, Rory could have decided not to persevere with his studies. Life was a constant struggle when he was growing up, caring for his mother and younger brother. But the family home, poor as it was, was a haven of warmth and laughter. His father had encouraged Rory to re-sit his exams after he received poor grades the first time round because he had been too tired to revise. No one had been prouder than Mr Grainger senior when his son had finally achieved his degree in business management.

Now seated at his desk, Rory ran a hand through his thick red hair. Tim Dalrymple was one of the best, a hard working employee who could turn his hand to anything, from changing a light bulb to dancing with a wallflower at the summer ball they held every year in aid of a local charity. In moments Tim could have the most nervous of ball guests relaxed and happy and thoroughly enjoying herself. He was a natural and everyone liked him.

Even though Tim had enjoyed a privileged upbringing so different from Rory's, he was not scared of getting his hands dirty. He was charming, hard working and pleasant, which was why Rory had let him take a few extra days of holiday even though the hotel and spa was fully booked for the next fortnight.

The Hills had received significant press publicity after an American singer had stayed with them during her time spent filming a costume drama on location at a nearby stately home. Her blog about the beauties of the country-side and the facilities on offer at the hotel had led to an avalanche of bookings.

Rory was not sure media types made the best clientele. Some could be very demanding and self centred — but not so Alison Matthews. She was an absolute sweetie and she was the reason why Rory had let Tim extend his leave.

Alison's agent had booked her into The Hills knowing he could rely on their discretion not to leak her presence to the press. Alison played the lead in a television drama but, due to an unfortunate liaison in her personal life, she had been temporarily written out of the series.

Tim had broken one of The Hills' most rigid rules. He had become involved with a client, not an ordinary client, but Alison Matthews. If the news became public knowledge, the media would besiege The Hills.

If the incident had involved anyone else Rory would not have hesitated in dismissing the culprit on the spot. But Rory knew that Tim was different. He had proved time and again that he could be relied upon to be helpful and discreet, not only with the celebrity guests they frequently had, but with the staff too.

Nothing was too much trouble for Tim. Rory had called him up at midnight on more than one occasion when discretion had been of the essence. A regrettable incident regarding the teenage daughter of a high profile businessman, and her unsuitable escort, could easily have had a disastrous outcome if it had not been for Tim's delicate handling of the situation. There had been no whisper of the incident in the press and a scandal had been averted.

Even so — Rory made a steeple of his fingertips — Tim's absence could not go on for much longer. Now that Alison Matthews had left The Hills, it was high time that Tim returned.

Bill had every right to complain

about his prolonged absence. And Rory also needed Tim Dalrymple back at work — as of now!

His hand hovered over the telephone but before he could pick it up to make his call, it rang.

'Mr Grainger?' a female voice enquired.

'What can I do for you?' he asked after he had identified himself.

'My name is Fiona Dalrymple.'

'Did you say Dalrymple?' Rory picked up on her name.

'Yes. I understand my brother is employed at The Hills.'

'I'm afraid we can't answer personal questions,' he replied smoothly.

'I wasn't aware I had actually asked one,' the caller replied crisply.

After a few moments of awkward silence Rory asked pleasantly. 'May I know the reason for your call?'

'I wish to speak to my brother but I seem to have been put through to you.'

'Your brother?' Rory repeated slowly. 'Well, Miss Dalrymple, perhaps you would like to leave me your number?'

'I was wondering if I could call in and see him?'

'You're very welcome to look around The Hills.' Rory did not miss a beat even though his suspicions were on full alert. Whoever this Fiona Dalrymple was, she was not Tim's sister.

Tim had told Rory his only relations were his grandparents. Rory strongly suspected the caller was a journalist who had somehow got wind of the affair between Alison Matthews and Tim Dalrymple. His lips tightened. If that were the case this 'Fiona Dalrymple' would get short shrift from Rory.

'Very well,' she said, 'would Wednesday afternoon be convenient?'

Rory flicked over the pages of the leather-bound diary on his desk.

'Three o'clock?' He made a note of the time. 'I'll look forward to seeing you.'

Rory replaced the receiver and glanced out over the manicured lawns, a frown of concentration creasing his brow. He didn't want to make the wrong decision, but as far as he knew Tim had lost his parents in a crash when he had been a child. His grandparents had brought him up and there had never been any mention of a sister.

Rory glanced at the calendar. Today was Friday. He hoped Tim would be back by next Wednesday. After all the inconvenience his absence from work had caused, Rory decided he could sort this Fiona person out.

'Time for the staff meeting.' The senior receptionist popped her head round Rory's office door. 'We're all ready.'

Dismissing all thoughts of Fiona Dalrymple from his mind, Rory headed out the office for his meeting.

4

'Frank says I'm over-reacting.' Ellie's words rang in Fiona's head as she drove along. She still hadn't come to terms with the shock of learning she actually had an older brother. Her sunny smile slipped. As a child she had always longed for a companion and had envied her classmates who all seemed to have brothers and sisters to play with.

Living with her grandparents, life had been quiet. The only time she could remember anything of excitement happening was when her grandmother discovered her grandfather was going on one of his sprees, usually to Europe and often without his wife. His pleas that it was a business trip normally fell on deaf ears . . . the usually mild Doreen could be very angry indeed when roused.

But for all that Fiona's childhood had

been happy, if a bit lonely.

After her grandfather's death when Fiona had been a teenager the light seemed to have gone out of her grandmother's life and she withdrew into herself. That was when Fiona had developed her love of gardening. Working in the open air gave her something to do on the long summer evenings when her grandmother was resting.

'Tell me something about Tim,' Fiona had asked Ellie who was sitting opposite her in the trimmed garden, looking as nervous as a kitten.

'I'll get you a photo,' she said.

The framed picture showed a rather serious looking young man staring back at the camera with the suggestion of a challenge in his eyes.

'He doesn't like having his photo taken,' Ellie explained with a light laugh. 'All because of that silly little scar under his eye. Can you see it there?' She tapped a manicured finger-nail on a tiny mark on Tim's cheek. 'He fell out of a tree as a boy and landed rather badly. The cut needed four stitches.'

'When was this taken?'

'Hmm?' Ellie looked up. 'I'm not sure. It may have been when he was at university. No I'm wrong, it was just before his eighteenth birthday party.'

'How old would that mean that Tim is now?' Fiona asked, instantly curious.

'Twenty-six.'

'That makes him three years older than me.'

'Yes?' Ellie sounded hesitant.

'Wouldn't he have remembered having a baby sister?'

A far away look came into Ellie's eyes. 'He did keep asking about you to begin with,' she admitted, biting her lip. 'In the end Frank simply told him you were with your parents.'

'You told Tim I was dead?' Fiona was outraged.

'No.' Ellie looked shocked. 'Frank thought it would be best if . . . well, he forgot about you . . . and after a time he did.'

'And so did you!' Fiona retorted.

'I've already explained all that, dear.'

Privately Fiona decided Ellie Marsden was a weak woman, easily browbeaten by her husband, a husband who preferred playing a round of golf to staying in to meet his step-granddaughter for the first time in over twenty years.

'All you've explained to me so far is that you walked out on your husband, my grandfather, taking your daughter with you. Then you separated me from my brother, told him I was dead and successfully managed to keep us apart for over twenty years.'

Her words had robbed Ellie's face of every vestige of colour.

'Fiona . . . I . . . ' Ellie produced a fine linen handkerchief from the pocket of her skirt and dabbed at her eyes. After a few moments she blew her nose defiantly. 'I suppose it was like that,' she admitted. 'Frank didn't want me to write to you after we saw Doreen's obituary notice in the newspaper, but I decided the time was right, so I wrote to you without his knowledge, or his approval.'

Fiona felt the first stirrings of respect for Ellie, albeit somewhat reluctant.

'That's why I'm so upset Tim isn't here to meet you. I've been telephoning his place of work on and off for days but he's not there. He always contacts me every day, either by text or email. I'm so worried I don't know what to do.

'I'm sure something's happened to him. I would have driven up to The Hills myself, it's not far, but Frank needs the car for his golf and I'm without transport.'

Fiona could not believe what she was hearing. Were there still women around so completely under their husband's thumb as Ellie Marsden? Obviously there were. Ellie was living proof of it.

'If I could arrange some time off work,' Fiona began, 'maybe I could drive to this . . . what was it? The Hills?'

'It's an exclusive hotel and spa. Perhaps you've heard of it? Frank and I had a meal there once. It's very pleasant.'

'It's also slightly out of my price range,' Fiona replied, recalling certain articles she'd read after an American superstar had sung its praises in the press.

Fiona's grandmother's idea of a good evening out was the occasional trip to the seaside and a fish supper on the pier. Her lips twitched as she wondered what Ellie Marsden's reaction to that sort of invitation would be. She could hardly believe the two women were so very different. The only thing they seem to have had in common was that they had both been married to Angus Weir. Unlike Ellie, Doreen was sweet and innocent, yet she too had covered up the fact that Fiona had a brother. Why all the family secrecy? It wasn't as if there was any scandal attached to their existence. It was only the death of their parents in a road accident that had separated Fiona and Tim — that and the machinations of two grandmothers.

Fiona shook her head. Whatever had gone on between the two women the night Mrs Shaw had stumbled on the drama in Rose Cottage all those years ago, it was all in the past, and life had to move on.

'Would you?' Ellie Marsden gushed. 'Drive up to The Hills, I mean? It's not far from the Sussex coast. I could give you a letter of introduction to the manager? His name is Rory Grainger.'

'Why don't you come with me?' Fiona suggested. 'We could make a little break of it and get to know each other a bit better?'

'I don't think I'll be able to come.'

'Because Frank wouldn't approve?' Fiona arched an eyebrow as her reluctant respect for her grandmother was beginning to evaporate.

Ellie lowered her eyes. 'It hasn't been easy.' Her voice was not much more than a whisper and for a moment Fiona felt as if she had forgotten her granddaughter was there.

'Give me the details,' Fiona said

briskly, deciding it would do no good pushing Ellie into something she really did not want to do. 'And I'll see what I can arrange.'

'Would you, dear? I would be so grateful.'

Ellie's look of pathetic relief was enough to convince Fiona she had made the right decision.

So it was that Fiona found herself driving along looking for the tiny Surrey hamlet of Hillside. It was proving difficult to find. Her satellite navigation system had insisted she should turn left down what appeared to be a cart track. When she had driven up and down the road three times, she decided it was the cart track or nothing. She bumped along for a few metres, before the trees cleared to reveal a beautiful valley.

She caught her breath at the sight that met her eyes. Nestled in the depths of the valley was a huge Victorian house. It was built along the lines of a miniature palace and must have taken an army of workers to look after it.

So this was The Hills. Fiona bit her lip. She had in her handbag her grandmother's letter of introduction to Rory Grainger. He hadn't sounded exactly friendly on the telephone and Fiona wondered if he knew more than he was prepared to say about Tim's disappearance. For one mad moment Fiona wondered if this Rory Grainger had injured Tim in some way, or worse, then she decided her imagination was getting the better of her. All the same, his disappearance was worrying and if Fiona didn't get the answers she was looking for she was going to contact the police.

There was only one way to find out what had happened to her brother, and that was by visiting The Hills. Putting her car in gear, Fiona inched her vehicle slowly forwards towards a rather impressive looking wrought-iron security gate.

The railings stared back at her. There were no guards or security personnel on duty. There wasn't even a sign indicating this was The Hills, but Fiona had keyed in the correct postcode and her satellite navigation had indicated that she had arrived. She thumped the steering wheel in frustration. What on earth did their guests do to get in? Flipping open her handbag for her mobile she was about to dial the hotel's number when she heard the roll of car tyres behind her.

Glancing in the driver's mirror she saw a sleek silver saloon easing towards her. Fiona jumped out of her car and approached the new arrival. The driver looked at her with enquiring eyes. They were very dark brown. He also had a healthy thatch of fox-red hair. George Ross, Fiona's ex-fiancé, had been red-haired with brown eyes. Fiona felt her smile of greeting tighten, then told herself she was being silly. Not all red-haired, brown-eyed men were like George Ross.

'Hello,' she greeted the man. 'Do you know if this is The Hills?'

'It is.' His reply was crisp. 'And you are?'

She hesitated. He was looking at her as if she had no right to be here, yet as far as she knew they weren't on private property. Uneasily aware that they were however in a remote part of the forest she said, 'My name is Fiona Dalrymple. I've come to visit my brother at The Hills, only,' she shrugged, indicating the lack of reception, 'there doesn't seem to be anyone around.'

'That's because this is the staff entrance. We all have a private number to key into that security box over there.'

He pointed to a discreet box hidden by an overgrown branch.

'No wonder I couldn't see it,' Fiona laughed. 'I was beginning to think The Hills must be pretty exclusive if even the guests can't gain access.'

'It is,' the man admitted. 'We don't let in the press.'

'I'm sure you don't,' Fiona murmured, not sure what had prompted that remark. 'But if you're a member of staff, is it against the rules for you to let me in on your staff card, or will I have to drive around to the main entrance?'

'You won't need to do either.'

'I beg your pardon?'

'My name is Rory Grainger.'

Fiona's brow cleared. 'You're the General Manager? We spoke on the telephone. I'm Fiona Dalrymple.' She reintroduced herself. 'As you may recall I've come to visit my brother, Tim.'

'Have you? Tell me, Miss Dalrymple, when did you last see your brother?'

'It was quite a while ago,' she began, evading a direct answer. Exactly what had she had stumbled into? This man was looking at her as if she were the purveyor of some particularly virulent disease.

'Can you tell me anything about your brother?' Rory asked.

'Not a lot, no,' Fiona confessed.

'Do you know the colour of his hair? His eyes? When is his birthday?'

'What is all this?' Fiona demanded,

beginning to grow annoyed.

'I thought so.' Rory's mouth was set in a grim line.

'What do you mean?'

'You're not Tim Dalrymple's sister are you?' he said with deep suspicion.

'Of course I am. Why would I pretend otherwise?'

'He doesn't have a sister. His only living relatives are his grandparents.'

'Look, we can't talk here,' Fiona began.

'I'm afraid we can't talk at all, Miss Dalrymple. I suggest you go back the way you came and spread the word amongst your colleagues that they are not welcome at The Hills. Neither do I welcome people trying to gain admittance by false pretenses.'

Fiona gaped, then gathered her wits. 'I don't know what's bugging you, Mr Grainger,' she began, 'all I want to do is talk to Tim and if you don't let me into the hotel I'm going straight to the police.'

'Do what you like. We don't welcome

members of the press at The Hills and you'll get no sympathy from the police if you spin them a pack of lies.'

'I don't work for the newspapers!' Fiona could not believe what she was hearing. 'What exactly is going on here? Have you got something to hide? Is that it? Is that why you don't want me to visit my brother?'

'I've told you. We don't welcome . . . '

'For your information I am not an undercover reporter. I work in my local library and I've taken time off especially to be here today. We had an appointment if you remember.'

'Then I suggest you go back to your library — if it even exists.'

'How dare you talk to me like that?' Fiona fumed. 'Tim Dalrymple is my brother. I have a letter from his grandmother in my bag, and,' she remembered the photo Ellie had showed her, 'he has a scar under his eye which he got after a childhood fall from a tree. It needed four stitches. Is that enough information for you, Mr

50

Grainger? Or perhaps you'd care to take my fingerprints and have them double checked by the police?'

Rory's brown eyes moved slowly up and down Fiona's body. She clenched her hands tightly into her sides, fighting down the urge to lash out at him.

'I suggest, Mr Grainger, that the reason you don't want the press here is because my brother has gone missing and you don't know where he is. So if you don't let me in, I really will go to the papers and I'll tell them all I know.'

She tilted her chin and waited for his reaction. She didn't have to wait long.

With a curt, 'Follow me,' he keyed his personal number into the security box.

Moments later the gates eased open. Rory drove his car through, leaving Fiona to follow quickly behind him before they closed shut again.

★   ★   ★

'Hello? Mrs Shaw?'

Fiona had taken refuge in the water

garden of The Hills, enjoying the late afternoon sunshine and trying to get her head round all that had happened since she had arrived a few hours ago.

'Fiona, dear, how lovely to hear from you.' Her neighbour's friendly voice at the other end of the line was strangely reassuring. 'So, you've arrived safely have you, then? I do hope you're having a good time?' she asked pointedly.

'I'm fine. I called because I'll be staying away for a few days and I wondered if you'd keep an eye on things for me at home?'

'Of course. Don't worry about a thing. I'm so pleased you took my advice about having a little holiday. I always say to my Jim that there's nothing like a change of scenery for lifting the spirits. Where are you anyway?'

'I'm staying in the country,' Fiona said guardedly. Much as she liked Mrs Shaw, she didn't actually need to know where Fiona was and for the moment Fiona preferred to keep things that way.

'You've got my mobile number should you need to contact me haven't you?'

'Yes. I keep it with your spare set of house keys.' Fiona's neighbour sounded a little huffy. Mrs Shaw didn't like being kept in the dark but for all that Fiona knew she could be relied upon to keep her word to look after Rose Cottage. 'Would you like me to go in once a day and water your plants for you?'

'That would be lovely, thank you.'

Fiona clicked off before Mrs Shaw could ask any further questions then punched in another number.

'Ellie? It's me, Fiona.'

'Hello, Fiona.' Her voice was little above a whisper as if she didn't want to risk being overheard.

'Is Frank there?' Fiona asked.

'Yes. Is there anything I can do for you?'

A dimple dented Fiona's cheek. She had a wild urge to ask for a home delivery of groceries. Playing cloak and dagger was not her style and in Fiona's opinion it was time Ellie stood up for herself to Frank.

'I was calling to update you on things here at The Hills.'

'Oh yes?' There was a quickening in Ellie's voice. 'Hold on I'll close the door. Frank is watching the racing on the television. He's in a bad mood because his golf has been cancelled.' There was a brief pause and the sound of movement down the other end of the line. 'Now, fire away,' Ellie said sounding a little breathless, 'I'm all ears.'

'I didn't start off on a very good foot with Mr Grainger,' Fiona began.

'Why's that?'

'He thought I was from the press.'

'How extraordinary.'

'That's what I thought.'

'Why should he think that, I wonder?'

'I think it's because he knows something about Tim's whereabouts but whatever it is, he's not letting on.'

'When Frank and I attended a

function at the hotel a little while ago he struck me as a most charming man. I can't believe he could possibly be involved in Tim's disappearance.'

Fiona's lips twisted in a wry smile. She suspected Rory Grainger would be perfectly charming to the guests, they were his bread and butter, but unimportant library assistants did not merit his charm.

'Well, I don't have witnesses, but until I produced your letter of introduction, and told him about Tim's scar, he wouldn't believe I was Tim's sister and was on the point of ejecting me off the premises.'

'This is most inconvenient. Would you like me to speak to him, dear? I could clear up any misunderstanding and assure him you really are my granddaughter.'

'That won't be necessary, thanks, Ellie. I managed to convince him in the end that I am who I say I am.'

Fiona tossed her dark hair out of her eyes remembering their robust exchange of views on the subject once they reached the hotel.

'Have you found anything out about Tim?' Ellie asked with a note of concern.

'Not so far. I'm staying in his room and tonight I'm due to have supper with one of the staff, so I'll start asking questions. Have you heard anything?'

'Not a word. It's so unlike him. I do hope nothing's happened to him. You will keep in touch and take care, won't you, Fiona dear? I would hate anything to happen to you as well.'

After assuring Ellie she would on both counts, Fiona rang off.

Her interview with Rory Grainger had not gone well. After accusing her of being a reporter, he had then demanded to know why she should suddenly come looking for her brother, twenty years after they had last met.

'Because my grandmother died,' she began to explain.

'If you are Tim's sister,' Rory had been quick to point out, 'you'd know your grandmother is very much alive.'

'I had two grandmothers. My grandfather married twice, not that his personal life is any of your business.'

Fiona faced up to Rory Grainger. She was blowed if this bully was going to intimidate her. Her breath was coming in short sharp bursts and she knew her face probably resembled a beetroot. She always coloured up when she was stressed and this man was enough to stress a saint.

The expression in Rory's brown eyes shifted slightly into reluctant respect as Fiona squared up to him. 'Point taken,' he acknowledged, 'but I'm still not convinced you are who you say you are.'

'Mr Grainger . . . ' She sighed in exasperation.

'Rory, please, and may I call you Fiona?'

She ignored the invitation to use his first name. 'I don't know why you don't want me here and to be honest I don't care. I didn't come to visit you anyway, but if you really want to get rid of me then the sooner you start answering my questions, the sooner I'll leave.'

'Are you sure you aren't a reporter?' he asked with a disarming smile. 'You'd make a very good investigative journalist.'

'I've told you before, I'm Tim's sister. My grandmother — the one who is still alive,' she added pointedly, 'is worried because he hasn't contacted her.'

'I see.' There was the faintest flicker of unease in Rory's smile. 'I have been in touch with Mrs Marsden, of course and if I do hear anything from Tim, I'll let her know immediately.'

'Aren't you worried that a reliable member of your staff has disappeared?'

'I'm not sure that he has,' Rory replied.

'He's been gone ten days.'

'Three days actually. He took a week's holiday. I was expecting him back on Sunday but it's not unknown for staff to get confused over their shift patterns. We have to work a twenty-four-seven rota system here. Tim may have thought he wasn't due back on duty until the end of the week.'

'Three days or ten, he should still be back by now.'

Rory paused before saying, 'Actually it's a bit of a delicate situation.'

'Is Tim in some sort of trouble?'

'I didn't say anything to Mrs Marsden when she rang to speak to Tim because it's up to Tim to tell her.'

'Has Tim done something wrong?' Fiona swallowed down a new fear.

'I gave him leave of absence because he was getting too involved with a guest and I needed to diffuse the situation.'

Fiona widened her eyes in surprise. 'A guest here at The Hills?'

'A high profile guest.'

'Is that allowed — getting involved?'

'It's strictly against the rules actually and he was very lucky to have only received a verbal warning.'

'Surely Tim wouldn't go off in a huff as a result of this involvement, would he?' Fiona asked.

'It would be very unlike him if he had. The guest concerned has since checked out so I have no way of checking if they are still an item. I sincerely hope the affair has fizzled out.'

'May I know who this high profile guest is?'

'We don't reveal the names of our guests and it's no good looking at me like that, Fiona. You won't hear it from me. In this business the first lesson you learn is how to be discreet.'

Fiona chewed her lip. She could understand Rory's point but all the same it was very frustrating.

'Can I see Tim's room? Is that allowed? I may be able to pick up some clues.'

'Feel free. You can stay over if you like as long as you don't harass the staff.'

'I just want to find my brother.' Fiona swallowed a lump in her throat that was threatening to distort her voice. 'Would you like me to sign some sort of disclaimer? I swear am not from the newspapers and I won't bully the staff. How's that for starters?'

'Very good,' Rory's slow smile transformed his face, 'and I'll take your word for it, there's no need to sign anything. I'll get one of the cleaners to take you over to the staff block.'

'Thank you,' Fiona replied as Rory reached for the telephone.

'I wouldn't want you to think I was being uncooperative,' Rory said. 'We've nothing to hide.'

As Fiona watched him punch in a telephone number she couldn't shake off the feeling that Rory Grainger wasn't telling her all he knew.

5

Monica sat down opposite Fiona and unscrewed the cap of her drink. 'So you're Tim's sister? You don't look like brother and sister.'

'Don't we?' Fiona raised an eyebrow. Monica had her at a disadvantage. Apart from the photograph Ellie had shown her, she didn't really know what Tim looked like. She began to wish she'd gone through her grandmother's suitcase of personal papers to see if there were any photograph albums amongst the bits and pieces she had collected over the years.

From what she could remember, Tim's hair was more of a sandy colour than her dark brown and his eyes were blue. He had been scowling at the camera in Ellie's photograph so it was difficult to guess what his smile was like.

'It's a shame he's not here, especially as you've come to visit him especially. Fancy him forgetting,' Monica replied. 'He's a lovely person. I like Tim. I mean he's posh having been to boarding school and all that, but you'd never know. He's not afraid to get his hands dirty.' Monica giggled. 'Sorry, didn't mean to be rude. I mean if he's posh you are as well aren't you?' Monica frowned. ''Cept you sound different in the way you talk.'

'Do you know him well?' Fiona asked trying to rescue the poor girl from her obvious embarrassment.

She and Tim may be brother and sister but their social backgrounds could not have been more different. Fiona had gone to the village school then to the sixth form college. There was no money for private education or for university.

'Not really. I've only been here three months.' Monica looked happier again and began to eat her salad. 'I clean the south chalet bedrooms so our paths don't cross that much.'

'How long has Tim been here?'

'About eighteen months I think.'

'What does he actually do?'

'Don't you know?' Monica asked with a puzzled frown.

'We've been out of touch for a while,' Fiona replied. 'He was abroad, so we didn't see much of each other.'

Monica seemed to accept Fiona's explanation. 'Tim does just about everything. Someone told me he started off in the gardens and he still works in them from time to time, but we were short of staff or something one day so he stepped in to help Rory and he's been his unofficial right hand man ever since.'

She gave a shy smile. 'Working here has taught me that every day there are little unexpected dramas to take care of. Tim's great at that sort of thing.'

'Is that so?' Fiona sipped her tea.

'Course he still likes being outside, growing things, vegetables and flowers, even if he doesn't get much time for it these days. The head groundsman gets quite cross when Tim's called away. Says no one understands the kitchen garden like he does.'

At last, Fiona thought, she had found a connection. She loved her little cottage garden and it seemed as though Tim shared her love of gardening, a passion they had inherited from their mother, Gillian, Ellie's daughter.

'Do you have any idea where Tim is?'

Monica shook her head. 'We weren't that close. I mean we'd share a cup of tea if he happened to be having his break at the same time as me but that's as far as our relationship went. He's lead ever such an interesting life abroad, visiting all these weird and wonderful places with names that I can't pronounce. Still, you'd know all about that, wouldn't you?'

Fiona nibbled at her sandwich to cover her confusion. It was surprisingly tasty. The bread was soft and the filling generous. Monica's salad, too, looked crisp and freshly prepared.

The staff room was clean and airy with large glass windows that looked out over the lake. The owners of The Hills hadn't stinted when it came to looking after their workforce. Besides the canteen, there was a television lounge, a laundry room and a recreation area that housed a billiard table and a small computer section for personal use.

Their private accommodation was housed on the first floor. The rooms weren't large but they were comfortable conversions of an old stable block. They all had a small shower unit and she noticed Tim had a microwave in his room.

'Does Tim have a partner?' Fiona asked, wondering if he used the microwave for late night romantic snacks.

Monica hesitated. 'I don't know,' she admitted. 'There was some talk about a girlfriend but I don't know the details,' she finished in a hurried sort of mumble.

'Mr Grainger mentioned something about him being friendly with a high profile female guest?'

'Did he? I'm afraid I wouldn't know about that.' Monica averted her eyes.

'You don't know anything at all?'

'Perhaps you'd better ask Rory.' Monica looked over her shoulder as if to make sure they weren't being overheard. 'We're not allowed to say anything, you see. We have to sign something called a confidentiality clause. That means we aren't allowed to talk to anyone about who stays here or anything. Rory's hyper about the press gaining access to the grounds. I'd seen one or two reporters hanging around the place myself when that American actress was staying. They tried to talk to one or two of the staff but they didn't get anywhere. Rory's very hot on discretion.'

'But I'm family. I'm not interested in gossip, I'm trying to trace my brother who seems to have disappeared.'

Monica began to look uncomfortable. 'You could try asking Paula about him. She's been here a long time. She's one of the receptionists and I think Tim was quite friendly with her.'

'Thanks, I will.'

'I've got to go.' Monica stood up. 'I have to turn down the beds while the guests are having their evening meal. I hope you find out where Tim is. I expect he forgot he was due back on Sunday.'

'Yes, I'm sure it's something like that.'

Fiona smiled reassuringly at the girl as she left the staff room, then decided to try her luck with Paula on reception.

The main building was buzzing with guests enjoying a drink in the bar before choosing which of the restaurants they wanted to eat in that evening.

Fiona hesitated as Paula dealt with a query from a customer. She noticed the The Hills logo on her blouse. Everyone wore it, either on overalls or shirts or jackets. It was prominently displayed on the stationery items, and on the cloakroom towels. Fiona wondered what sort of uniform Tim wore. He was obviously at home in places like this and might even have visited as a guest with Ellie and Frank.

The highlights of Fiona's day in the library were usually finding a book they'd thought lost or helping with the adult literacy programme that she'd set up, not dealing with the tantrums of televisions stars.

Seeing Paula was now free, Fiona stepped forward and introduced herself.

'Sorry, couldn't say where he is, or what he's been up to,' Paula breezed back at Fiona with a professional smile when she'd gone on to ask about Tim. 'Fancy Tim having a sister. He never mentioned you. We must get together some time.' She turned away. 'Yes sir, can I help you?'

She switched her attention from Fiona back to a guest, leaving Fiona feeling that yet again she had been given the brush-off.

With a frown, she made her way back to Tim's room. She had hoped to find something amongst his things to give her a clue as to his whereabouts, but it was a very masculine room, basic and with very few personal possessions.

Fiona sat on the bed and wondered where Tim had lived before The Hills. From what she could gather from Ellie, she and Frank had returned home about eighteen months ago, and if what Monica said could be relied upon then that would coincide with the time Tim had been at The Hills.

A knock on the door made her jump. When she looked up Rory Grainger was standing in the corridor.

'Thought I might find you here,' he said with his pleasant smile. 'Paula and Monica said you'd spoken to them about Tim but that they couldn't help you.'

'Are you spying on me?' Fiona demanded.

'Actually I was wondering if you'd like to come out with me for a drink?'

'Now?'

'That was the idea.'

'Aren't you on duty?'

'I like to get off the premises every now and then. Someone always manages to find me if I try to relax in the staff room.' Rory looked at Fiona expectantly. 'Please say yes. I'm not allowed to ask members of staff out for a drink and it gets very lonely going out on your own.'

Privately Fiona thought Rory Grainger looked the sort of man who would have no trouble finding a female companion with whom he could pass his lonely evenings. Wondering if this was another ploy to see if she was a journalist in disguise, she decided to accept his offer. If he did know where Tim was he might let something slip and right now she needed all the help she could get.

★   ★   ★

The Surrey countryside looked beautiful in the early summer evening as Rory drove them out of Hillside through tiny villages nestling at the heart of the North Downs. Sometimes it was difficult to believe they were in the twenty-first century as they passed through hamlets consisting of two cottages and a church.

'What part of the country do you come from?' she asked as the silence between them lengthened.

He cast her a sideways glance. 'Can't you tell?' he said. 'I'm a scouser, born and bred in Liverpool.'

'I . . . er, no. Never been very good at accents.' Fiona had actually only been making polite conversation but now she came to think about it, Rory did sound like some of the pop groups from the sixties. Her grandfather always played that sort of music, very loudly; sometimes, Fiona suspected, just to annoy her grandmother who was more into light classical.

'You're smiling. Are Liverpudlians funny?'

'I was thinking about my grandfather, actually,' Fiona admitted.

'You can tell me about him inside,' Rory said as they drew into the car park of a thatched roof pub.

'There's not much to tell really,' Fiona said as they settled down with their drinks. She noticed Rory drank orange juice, like she did. 'He was a lawyer, a very good one. His work often took him abroad.'

'So that's why Tim went to boarding school?'

'Is it? I mean . . . ' Fiona hesitated. 'How much do you actually know about my brother?' she asked, suspecting Rory may well be trying to trip her up again.

'Why don't you tell me what you know?'

Rory's voice was soft and if Fiona hadn't known better she would have suspected his interest was genuine.

'I was a baby when our parents were killed in a car crash. Tim was — I mean, is — three years older than me.' Fiona sipped some juice to ease the dryness in her throat. 'Look, I know you're not going to believe a word I say, but it is the truth. Until a few days ago, I didn't even know I had a brother.'

'That explains why Tim didn't mention you,' he said. 'I presume he didn't know about you either?'

'That's just it. I think he did. It's complicated but my grandfather was married twice. He and his first wife are my proper grandparents, my mother's parents.'

'I'm with you so far,' Rory said, managing to be both friendly and guarded.

'My grandfather married again after his first marriage broke down. After my parents' accident, I stayed with my grandfather and his second wife. Tim went abroad with his first wife and her new husband.'

'Fine.' Rory looked thoughtful. 'So why was there no contact between you and your brother?'

'They told Tim I was with my parents, dead.' She caught the flash of surprise in Rory's eyes. 'Please, don't say anything,' she stopped him from speaking, 'it really is none of your business.'

'Fair enough,' he conceded, 'although it's quite a story. Am I permitted to ask another question?'

'As long as I don't have to answer it?' Fiona felt an enormous sense of relief now Rory knew the truth. It was easy to talk to him and she could understand why he was so popular with his employees.

'How did you find out? And why have you only just tried to contact him.'

'That's two questions.'

'You choose which you want to answer.'

'My grandmother died and my grandfather's first wife sent a letter of condolence. She invited me over for tea. When I went to see her she dropped the bombshell about me having a brother and that he would have been there to join us for tea only he had gone missing.'

'Wow.' Rory drained his drink.

'That's some family you've got.'

'I expect there are skeletons in your family cupboard too.'

'I expect there are,' he agreed.

'So what are we going to do about Tim? Should we contact the police?'

'The police?'

'Isn't that what you normally do when someone goes missing?'

'I'm sure he's not missing.'

'Why? Do you know where he is?' Without realising it Fiona had put her hand on his arm. The muscles were firm under her fingers. She removed her hand quickly. 'Because if you do, and you don't want to tell me, then tell his grandmother because she is worried sick about him.'

'I can't do that,' Rory admitted.

'Can't or won't?' Fiona said sullenly, her resentment resurfacing quickly.

'I'm sure Tim will be back within the next few days. Until then you're very welcome to stay on.'

'Yes, but if no one will talk to me, what am I going to do?'

'Actually didn't you say you work in a library?'

'Yes.'

'You could help out in the office if you like. The paperwork's in a bit of a mess. It could do with tidying up.'

'Aren't you scared I might stumble on some private information and sell it to the tabloids?' Fiona demanded, still smarting from Rory's refusal to tell her where Tim was.

'I keep all my private stuff hidden away from prying eyes. So unless you know the combination to the safe you won't be able to get at them. Interested?'

'I might be.' Fiona was not prepared to totally commit. Whatever information Rory was keeping from her, she wished he would trust her enough to share it.

This time it was Rory who put a hand out to touch hers. 'I promise you there's nothing to worry about. Nothing has happened to Tim and this time next week you'll be wondering what all the fuss was about.'

'I hope so.'

'You don't sound very positive.'

'You know, I used to think my life was dull, going to the library every day then working on my garden in my spare time. Then after my grandmother died, I learned she wasn't my grandmother. My real grandmother tells me I have a brother and that brother has disappeared.' Fiona spoke quickly to ease the tightness in her throat.

'I am sure Tim will be overjoyed to find you again,' Rory said gently. 'I've got a younger brother and I always look out for him. I'm sure Tim will look out for you, too. He's like that, you know. You're a lucky girl to have such a brother.'

'So you believe I am Tim's sister now?'

'Oh yes. Your grandmother loves you very much. She was so worried about you she telephoned me this evening. She gave me a bit of an earful actually. I'm sorry I mistook you for a journalist.

I was out of order.'

Fiona blinked in surprise. People had often told her that her grandmother loved her very much, but they had been referring to Doreen. To hear from Rory that Ellie felt the same way about her was a surprise.

Rory glanced at his watch. 'If you've finished your drink we'd better be getting back. I like to do a final round of the premises before we close the facilities for the evening.'

Fiona saw with surprise almost three hours had passed. Three hours in which Rory had given her his full attention and in those three hours she was also surprised to realise she had not once thought about George Ross.

'So, do we have a date in the office for ten o'clock tomorrow morning?'

As Fiona fell asleep in Tim's bed listening to the night sounds from the garden she found herself looking forward to the next morning and the challenges the day would bring.

6

Mrs Shaw called out of her upstairs window to where the visitor was standing on Doreen's front doorstep. 'Can I help you?'

The sandy-haired young man glanced up to see where the voice was coming from. 'I'm looking for Mrs Doreen Weir.'

'Doreen?' Mrs Shaw repeated in shock. 'You're sure it's Doreen you want?'

'This is her house? Rose Cottage? Is this where Doreen Weir lives?'

'Er, yes.'

'Do you know where she is?' he asked.

'I'll come down.' Mrs Shaw closed her window and hurried downstairs. 'There's no one in at the moment,' she explained, breathing heavily.

Mrs Shaw wasn't used to rushing,

but she sensed this visitor might be worth investigating — and possibly have something to do with Fiona's absence and she didn't want him disappearing before she had a word with him. She hadn't totally believed her young neighbour's explanation that she was staying with friends in the country. Her instinct told her that something was going on, and when strange men came knocking at Doreen's door asking to speak to her late neighbour then she wanted to know about it.

'Is Mrs Weir away?' he asked.

'May I know why you want to see her?' Mrs Shaw hedged, playing for time.

'It's a personal matter,' the young man replied.

'Is it indeed? Well, as I explained there's no one here at the moment.'

'Are you expecting her back soon?'

Mrs Shaw shook her head. 'No.'

'Then I'll call again later in the week.'

'What name shall I say?'

It was only with the greatest of

restraint that Mrs Shaw did not put out a hand and physically detain him until she found out exactly what his business was with Rose Cottage, but the expression on his face, while not exactly unfriendly, did not invite confidence.

'Do you really not know when she'll be back?' The young man's face was screwed up in concern and Mrs Shaw's heart went out to him.

'You do mean Doreen?' Mrs Shaw wanted to clarify that point. Her hearing wasn't all it should be some days.

'Yes.'

'I'm not sure.' Mrs Shaw sensed the young man's impatience with her. The truth was she knew more about Doreen than anyone, apart from Angus and she wished she didn't. 'I have a contact telephone number for — er, emergencies, so I could pass on any message, if you like?'

'May I have it? The number that is?' he asked a little too eagerly.

'Who did you say you were again?'

The young man ran a hand through his hair in an agitated manner. It was clear he thought he was talking to a rather slow-witted neighbour. Mrs Shaw was glad she couldn't make out exactly what he was muttering under his breath.

'Is anything wrong?' she asked in concern.

He shook his head. 'No. Nothing.' He looked away from her as if he had forgotten her presence. Clearly he thought she could be of no further use to him. 'I'll . . . er, thank you. Thank you,' he seemed to remember his manners and smiled. 'I'll call again.'

'You still haven't told me who you are.' Mrs Shaw gave it one last try, but he didn't turn back or reply.

She watched him go, frowning. There was something about the man that was vaguely familiar, but she couldn't put her finger on it. In his casual outfit he didn't look like a housebreaker and he would hardly have been knocking on Doreen's door if he was, but you never knew these days, she thought.

Perhaps she ought to check that everything was in order next door in case he was casing the joint. She picked up Fiona's keys off the hook and, hurrying across to Rose Cottage, unlocked the door, wrinkling her nose at the musty smell that greeted her. She bent down to pick up several letters off the mat. The photo of Fiona smiled back at her from its place of honour on the hall table as Mrs Shaw placed the letters next to it. She had seen the photograph so many times but today it drew more than a casual passing glance.

Fiona was wearing one of her gardening tee shirts and smiling, as she held up her prize-winning marrow from the local summer fair. It was the sort of photograph that always made you smile. Fiona had been so thrilled with her cup and she and Mrs Shaw had taken it to the jewellers in town to have her name engraved on it.

Mrs Shaw caught her breath in surprise. Her eyes were deceiving her. She picked up the photograph to study it further. The resemblance to the young man who had just called was unmistakable. He and Fiona had the same slightly shy smile and, here Mrs Shaw knew she was being silly, but their hands looked exactly the same. Fiona's were clasped around her monster marrow and Mrs Shaw had noticed the young man's hands when he'd run them through his hair. Fiona's fingers were long and thin as were those of the recent visitor to Rose Cottage, and now Mrs Shaw came to think of it she could see a definite facial resemblance between the two of them.

Forgetting about watering the plants, Mrs Shaw relocked Rose Cottage and hurried next door to leave a message Fiona's voicemail.

* * *

'It's quite a simple filing system and can be done in seconds.' Rory smiled at Fiona. 'Although you wouldn't believe it would you?' He gave an embarrassed shrug towards the piles of paperwork on his assistant's desk. 'What I would like you to do is to file the receipts in those ring binders in alphabetical order. I haven't had time to get round to it.'

'Working in a library you get good at putting things in alphabetical order,' Fiona replied as she put down her bag and took off her coat, 'and making order out of chaos.'

'Did you have a nice walk?' he asked.

'Lovely. Thank you.'

The morning mist hadn't been completely burnt off by the sun and there had been a chill in the air as Fiona took her early morning stroll around the rose garden. The smells of damp grass and crushed petals made her feel homesick for Rose Cottage. The Hills was a beautiful hotel but it did nothing for her.

Her holidays had always been of the budget variety. Whenever they could afford it, she and her grandmother always spent a few days in Cornwall at a tiny bed and breakfast near Truro. For two idyllic weeks they would enjoy everything the Cornish coast had to offer, for a fraction of the cost of a stay at The Hills.

Good fresh air, mouth-watering food and the pleasure of each other's company had been all Fiona and her grandmother wanted to enjoy themselves.

Fiona recalled how George had turned up his nose at the idea of a honeymoon in Cornwall. He preferred a place with a high nightlife and lots of energetic water sports.

Fiona realised in surprise it was so long since she had thought about George Ross, she almost had difficulty remembering what he looked like.

'Why the sad expression?'

Rory's voice drew her out of her thoughts as he settled down opposite Fiona.

'It's nothing really,' she insisted.

'Anything you want to talk about? I'm a very good listener.'

When he wasn't accusing her of being an undercover news reporter,

Rory Grainger displayed another side to his character, someone who cared. Fiona liked the way his eyes softened at the corners when he smiled and he was clearly a big hit with all the staff. She hadn't heard one bad word about him.

If only she could shake off the sneaking suspicion that he was hiding something from her she might feel better about him too. Perhaps that was why he had been so rude to her on her first day here — to get her to leave. She straightened her back. If Rory Grainger thought a few rude words were going to frighten Fiona Dalrymple then he had made a big mistake.

'No thank you.' Fiona clicked open the A-F file with a crisp click and began inserting the relevant documents.

'As you wish.' Rory didn't look in the least chastened by her rebuff.

'Do you like gardening?' Rory asked conversationally.

'I love it,' Fiona enthused. Her face lit up as she added, 'In the summer I'm always working outside. June and July are my busiest months.'

'Tim likes gardening too.' Rory looked up from the schedule he was inspecting. His eyes widened as he took in Fiona's animated face and heightened colour as she talked about her garden. 'You'll have lots to discuss when you finally meet up.'

Rory cursed under his breath as he saw that his words had wiped the happiness from Fiona's face.

'Sorry, I didn't mean to mention Tim.'

'It's been two days now since I arrived and I'm still no nearer discovering where my brother is. Wouldn't you be worried if your brother went missing?'

'I have to admit I would.'

'Ellie Marsden is constantly leaving agitated messages on my mobile and as for Mrs Shaw . . . '

'Who's Mrs Shaw?'

'My next door neighbour. She's very nosy and she keeps asking awkward questions. I fobbed her off as best I could, but I'm sure she doesn't believe me. How did my life suddenly get so complicated?'

'A question I often find that I ask myself,' Rory admitted somewhat wryly.

The only member of staff who expressed any concern about Tim was Bill, the head groundsman.

'Best vegetable gardener I ever had,' he mumbled in reply to Fiona's queries about her brother. 'Can't understand him taking off like that. You find him, you hear?' He waggled his bushy eyebrows at Fiona. And send him back. Then I'll give him a piece of my mind for leaving us all in the lurch. In my day we got the sack if we took off without notice. Don't know what the world's coming to.'

Fiona knew it would do no good asking Rory any more questions. He always blanked her at the same time as professing to welcome her presence in the hotel.

She wondered what Rory would do if she threatened to call in the police again. With her head full of conflicting emotions, she worked quietly and efficiently for several moments.

'I can actually see across the room for the first time in ages.' Rory looked up as he signed off his schedule. 'Sure you don't want a permanent job here?'

Fiona shook her head. 'Filing records at a desk all day is not my scene.'

'Well don't feel you have to finish it all,' he said, glancing at his watch. 'I have to go out now.' He paused and Fiona noticed underneath his outdoor tan he'd gone rather red. 'I'd be pleased to treat you to dinner as a thank you for all your hard work and to make up for being so unwelcoming on your first day.'

Fiona noticed his Liverpudlian accent was more pronounced when he was unsure of himself. She hid a smile. Who would have thought it? Rory Grainger was nervous of asking her out to dinner.

'Filing is hardly hard work,' she said as she clicked the last sheet of paper into its allotted place, then she added, 'but you're right, you were appallingly rude to me the day we met so if you don't mind me probing you with questions about my brother then dinner would be great.'

A look of panic crossed Rory's face. 'I'm not sure I like the sound of that.' His pager bleeped, interrupting them. 'Seems I'm wanted poolside.' Rory slipped on his The Hills blazer and with a smile that until now Fiona thought he only reserved for important guests he left the office.

She slotted the file back into its correct place on the shelf. Rory Grainger would be her first date since George, and he had been her only boyfriend. They'd grown up together and sort of fallen into their engagement. Perhaps that was where they had gone wrong. Rory Grainger was a very different person to George. Maybe the time had come to move on.

Fiona glanced at the wall clock. If she was quick there might still be time to speak to the aromatherapist before her first appointment. One of the staff had said that she and Tim used to pal up on quiz night in the local pub.

The telephone rang as Fiona was searching out her bag.

'Library front desk,' she said without thinking.

'I beg your pardon?' a voice greeted her. 'I thought that was Rory's office.'

'Sorry! Yes, it is. I'm afraid Mr Grainger isn't here.'

'Not to worry. Can you take a message?' Fiona quickly snatched up a handy piece of paper and found a pen. 'Will you tell him I'm confirming that Alison Matthews will be with you tonight but she's been delayed? Filming has run on.'

'Alison Matthews?' Fiona repeated carefully.

'That's right. Her driver will be with you about half past nine tonight. I hope that's not too late?'

'No, that's fine,' Fiona said, automatically assuming it was. 'We'll look forward to seeing her later.'

Fiona sat on her bed in her nightdress sipping the cup of soup she had made in Tim's microwave. She sensed an uneasy presence every time she appeared in the staff room, so tonight she had missed supper. A quick search of Tim's cupboards revealed several cans of tomato soup and a tin opener.

Fiona was beginning to think she was wasting her time at The Hills. The aromatherapist had been as tight-lipped as the rest of the staff. All Fiona could get out of her was that she and Tim were the gardening and health experts on the local quiz team and that they had won the contest several times. She seemed more annoyed that he wouldn't be turning up for the final this week, than the fact that he was absent without leave.

Fiona flicked open her mobile to check her calls. Unsurprisingly, there were messages from Ellie and Mrs Shaw.

'Hello, dear.' Ellie's refined accent greeted her. She lowered her voice to its usual whisper. Frank was clearly in the vicinity. 'Have you any news yet? Please ring as soon as you can. I'm growing rather worried. Tim can be rather impetuous at times. I do hope he hasn't done anything silly. There was some talk about a girlfriend, but he didn't give me any details. Oh, by the way I had a word with Mr Grainger and told him I was most disappointed in the way he was treating you.'

Fiona bit her lip in frustration. What was wrong with Tim? If nothing else why on earth wasn't he contacting Ellie? It was only natural she would be worried sick when he didn't call her.

She clicked on to the second message.

'Fiona, dear, Nancy Shaw here. I've got some news. A young man called at Rose Cottage this morning and,' she paused for dramatic effect, 'he wanted to speak to Doreen. Of course I didn't tell him anything, but I thought you should know. I know you'll think I'm being silly but honestly, dear, he looked very like you in your photograph; you know, the one with the marrow? Anyway mustn't witter on. Having a nice holiday? Better go. I've got to get Jim's dinner on.'

The message had been left the previous lunchtime but this had been the first chance Fiona had to check her calls.

She hated to involve Mrs Shaw in her personal life but she did need to know more about the mystery caller. Could it possibly be Tim? Surely not. As far as Tim was concerned he didn't have a sister — unless Ellie had mentioned something to him. Was that the reason he had taken off?

She began to key in Mrs Shaw's number before she realised someone was tapping on the door. Fiona reached out for her dressing gown and shrugged it on over her nightgown.

'Timmy,' a voice hissed through the keyhole, 'let me in. I don't want to get caught lurking around the staff quarters. We got into enough trouble last time.' The female voice ended with a giggle. 'How did you get on? Did you manage to find out anything?'

Fiona opened the door carefully and confronted the caller. A beautiful blonde girl wearing a Hills bathrobe was hovering outside hopping from one foot to the other in agitation.

'Heavens, who are you?' She grimaced, then not waiting for an answer added, 'I'm really really not supposed to be here. I sneaked out of the sauna when no one was looking.' Her delicate teeth gripped her bottom lip. 'Sorry to disturb you. You don't know where Timmy is, do you? Has he moved rooms? I have to speak to him,' she gushed.

'You'd better come in,' Fiona said as she tried to get her head round this latest development.

She had never met Alison Matthews in her life but she recognised her instantly. Who wouldn't? She appeared on television several times a week as the nation's favourite troublemaker in a prime time soap opera. Her character had been written out after a drama in Alison's personal life, but such was her magnetism the producers had been forced to re-introduce her after the switchboard was bombarded with calls of outrage.

Viewers made a point of staying in to watch the latest episode of her shenanigans at the vet's practice where she worked. With her aristocratic looks and porcelain skin, she was the face of today. She was feisty, smart and sassy, so what was she doing knocking on Tim's door at midnight?

Alison closed the door very slowly and very quietly behind her and tiptoed gently into the room.

'You won't tell on me, will you?' The violet blue eyes pleaded. 'No one's supposed to know about Timmy and me. It's strictly against the rules for staff and guests to fraternise.'

'No, I won't tell,' Fiona assured her.

Alison looked round expectantly. 'Tim's not here,' Fiona explained.

'Where is he?' Alison asked.

'I was hoping you might have seen him recently,' Fiona said guardedly.

'Not since my last visit. I had to leave in a hurry,' Alison hesitated. 'I didn't get a chance to say a proper good bye.'

'Then you won't know he's disappeared?' Fiona asked.

'What?' Alison's delicately plucked eyebrows rose several centimetres. 'You're kidding.'

'I'm staying in his room while I try to find out where he is.'

'Look, what's going on?'

'It's a long story,' Fiona sighed. 'I don't know where to start.'

Alison perched on her bed. 'How about at the beginning?' She paused. 'By the way, do you recognise me?'

'Of course I do.' Fiona smiled back at Alison. No one could mistake the beauty with the cascading blonde hair and perfect rosebud mouth. She wasn't wearing any make-up but even with a face shiny from the sauna she still managed to look stunning. 'You're Horrible Harriet.'

'Courtesy of the tabloids. I'm not like that in real life, I promise.'

'No one could be that horrible,' Fiona smiled.

'You'd be surprised. Have you ever worked in a film studio?'

'No.'

'Tensions can run pretty high. Anyway . . . sorry, got distracted. I wasn't attention seeking by asking if you recognise me, what I mean is you promise you won't tell anyone about me being here?'

'I won't if you do me a favour in return.'

The wary look was back in Alison's deep blue eyes. 'What sort of favour?' she asked carefully.

'Tell me everything you know about Tim Dalrymple.'

'Why?' Her rosebud mouth formed a perfect circle. 'You're not a hotel detective are you?' she asked, horrified. 'Have I walked into a trap?'

'No. I'm Tim's sister, Fiona.'

'What?'

'Keep your voice down!' Fiona made silencing gestures with her hands.

'Sorry, forgot! But if you really are Timmy's sister, that's terrific because he's gone looking for you.'

'But he doesn't even know I'm alive.'

'Yes he does. His grandmother told him. They had the most terrific row about it.' Alison put a hand to her mouth. 'Is that why he's taken off? I thought he wasn't talking to me because I got him into trouble with the boss.'

'Do you mean Rory Grainger?'

'What other boss is there?'

'Then he knows all about this?'

'All about what?' Alison frowned.

'Tim looking for me.'

'I don't know. It's possible I suppose.'

'If he does,' Fiona's thoughts were racing away with her, 'that would explain why he doesn't want me to leave and why he won't let me contact the police.'

'The police? Now hold on ... '
Alison made to scramble off the bed,
but Fiona grabbed out at her wrist.

'Rory Grainger told me he gave Tim
seven days' leave but his return is way
overdue. He fobbed me off with some
story about shift patterns but I simply
don't believe him.'

'All this is my fault,' Alison admitted
with a miserable droop to her mouth.

'Why?'

'I know it sounds corny but it really
was love at first sight.' A delicate pink
hue stained Alison's delicate neck. 'I
went for an early morning walk, before
anybody else was up and about — or so
I thought. Timmy was in the rose
garden. He said it was his favourite
time of day, when the garden was just
waking up. The flowers smelt so
beautiful and ... oh dear,' Alison
lowered her eyes shyly.

'Go on,' Fiona urged her.

'When you're in my line of work, you
meet so many false people, people who
only want to know you for who you are

and what you can do for them, not because they like you. With Timmy it was different. Timmy was like a breath of fresh air. He made me laugh, not because I'm Alison Matthews, but because I'm me, an ordinary girl who grew up in a semi in Essex. He even calls me Jean, that's my real name — Jean Smith would you believe? Not very charismatic is it?'

Fiona put out a hand and squeezed Alison's fingers. Soap star or not, when it came to affairs of the heart, Alison Matthews was as vulnerable as any girl.

'Anyway, later on that day I was in the beauty salon, and I heard the aromatherapist chatting to that Paula from reception about the quiz night at the pub, and how she and Timmy were on the team and were in with a chance for a place in the final. I know I shouldn't have done, but I followed them down there. Bad move, I know, but I wasn't thinking straight. Of course I was spotted. People began taking photos on their mobiles and asking me for my autograph. My agent and Rory Grainger were not best pleased. My stay here was supposed to be a closely guarded secret.'

'I can imagine,' Fiona sympathised.

'I was hustled off the premises. I've been so worried about Timmy. I thought maybe something had happened to him because of me. I've left loads of texts on his mobile. I was so frantic I wangled another visit here because my last one was cut short.'

'When was your last contact with Tim?'

'About ten days ago. I thought when he didn't reply to my messages that things were over between us. That's why I'm here tonight, to try and get him to at least speak to me. If our relationship really is over then I want to hear it from him, not in a text.'

Fiona blinked. Her thoughts were whirring through her head like a reel of film. If what Alison said was true it was no wonder Ellie was worried. It was Ellie's fault Tim had disappeared. Was that why she had then contacted Fiona and told her about Tim? But it still didn't explain why Rory wasn't more worried about Tim — a key member of staff who was way overdue back from leave.

'You know you look like your brother,' Alison confided. 'I think it's something to do with the way you hold your head, somehow,' she said wistfully.

'My next door neighbour said someone called at my cottage yesterday and that he reminded her of me.'

'This is better than any soap plot I know.' Alison's face was alight with enthusiasm. 'Do you think you'd better go home in case this stranger calls again? And if he does and it is Timmy, you will tell me won't you?'

'I need to speak to my neighbour first and Ellie, Tim's grandmother. And Rory as well.' Fiona's lips tightened as she mentioned his name.

'So it's true about you and Timmy being split up as babies?'

'Yes. I stayed with one grandmother

and Tim went with the other.' Fiona did her best to keep her tangled personal circumstances simple.

'And you honestly never knew about each other, all that time?' she asked.

'No,' Fiona said sadly.

Alison screwed up her nose. 'That is weird.'

A noise in the corridor outside disturbed them.

'I'd better get back before someone discovers I'm missing.' Alison lowered her voice then she hugged Fiona. 'I'm so pleased we've met. Look, we'd better keep in touch. If you hear from Timmy will you promise to contact me? And if I get a message from him, I'll do the same. This is my personal number,' she scribbled it down on a scrap of paper, 'and this is the address of my flat. For heaven's sake keep them in a safe place. I know journalists who would kill for this information.'

'Do you think you should be giving it to me?' Fiona eyed the note uneasily, reluctant to take it from Alison.

'Right now you're my only contact with Timmy.' Alison's blue eyes filled with tears. 'I know I've got this reputation as a troublemaker, but honestly, it's not true and Timmy, he's like my spiritual other half. I don't think I could bear it if I never saw him again.'

Fiona's generous mouth curved into a smile of sympathy. For someone who was supposed to be so sophisticated, Alison was showing an alarming tendency to go all soppy on her. She was growing to like her more every second. Sitting on Tim's bed exchanging telephone numbers Alison Matthews had never looked less like a television star.

'If you've ever been in love you'll know what I mean,' Alison apologised.

'Yes,' Fiona echoed faintly, wondering why on earth the image of Rory Grainger should slip into her mind. She certainly wasn't in love with him.

'Time I made a move. Would you see if the coast is clear?' Alison whispered.

Fiona slipped off the bed and, opening her door, she peered up and down the corridor. There was no one in sight.

'All clear.' She beckoned Alison off the bed.

'Wish me luck.' Alison kissed Fiona on the cheek. 'I left the back door to the sauna open. I've probably let out all the heat. Hope I don't set the alarms off. Keep in touch.' She crossed her fingers at Fiona before scampering away down the stairs back to the safety of the sauna.

7

Fiona strolled over towards the main house, taking her usual detour via the rose garden. She hadn't wakened up until gone eight after all the drama of the night before. The staff bell had not stirred her from her deep slumber and when she finally made her way to the staff room, the only thing the canteen could offer was some burnt toast. After her interrupted supper, she was feeling very hungry.

'Any luck finding that brother of yours?' Bill called over with a wave in her direction as she walked through the garden.

'Still looking,' Fiona replied.

Bill muttered something under his breath that sounded like, 'Try looking harder,' before he stomped off into the kitchen garden.

Fiona took a few moments out to

look around at her surroundings. So this was the scene of Alison's meeting with Tim. She could understand her being seduced by the beauty of it all. It was quite the most magical place Fiona had ever been in. The main garden had obviously been made over by professionals, but this little corner reflected the true style of a cottage garden as a place where lovers should fall in love. There was a rose arbour and a trellis and a small fountain with a statue of Aphrodite in the middle.

Fiona made a wry face. While she was happy for Alison and Tim, she would not be falling in love again for a long time. The scars caused by George's defection were beginning to heal, but the memory of his deception ran deep.

She turned and made her way up to Rory's office. She would have to tell him she intended to go home later today. If the mystery caller at Rose Cottage had been Tim then she would need to be there if he called again before Mrs Shaw, with her unerring instinct for gossip, started firing questions at him.

After what Alison told her last night Fiona decided she would not tell Rory the true reason she was leaving. If he could have his secrets then so could she. Besides which she still wasn't completely sure she trusted him.

Rory was seated at his desk filling in a form. He glanced up at Fiona.

'Heaven preserve me from high profile guests, they manage to make so much paperwork.'

'Good morning, Rory,' Fiona greeted him.

Her smile received an answering twitch of his lips.

'Sorry,' he apologised, 'good morning, Fiona. Did you sleep well?'

'Passably.'

'Have you come to attack some more filing?'

The phone began ringing on his desk. Rory picked it up. 'No comment,' he said after a few moments and slammed down the receiver.

'What's the matter?' Fiona asked, taking in the deranged state of his desk. His hair was standing on end as well, as if he had run his hands through it numerous times in frustration.

'The press have got wind of Alison Matthews' stay here. They've been trying to book themselves in under false names and they have even tried to bribe several members of staff for information.'

'Actually I took the booking call from her agent yesterday,' Fiona informed him. 'I gave the details to the reception desk immediately and before you start accusing me of anything underhand, I did not inform the press that Alison Matthews was a guest here.'

'I never suspected you did,' Rory admitted with an embarrassed smile. 'All the same I wish the wretched girl hadn't come back.'

'You mean after all the trouble she caused with Tim?'

'How did you find out about that?'

Rory asked in a sharp voice.

'There was a picture of them together in one of the tabloids,' Fiona replied, thinking on her feet.

'I feared as much.' Rory accepted her explanation without question. 'That sort of thing unsettles our other guests. They like to come here for peace and quiet, complete rest and relaxation. They don't expect to be hounded by the press every time they poke their heads outside the door.' Rory half smiled. 'Who'd be a hotel manager?'

'Where's Alison now?'

'That's just it.' Rory held up the report. 'She's not here.'

'What?'

'She left very early this morning. Her agent called her back to London, big drama at the studios or something. I've got to fill in an incident log and send it to head office in case there are any repercussions — and all this for a stay of less than twelve hours.'

Fiona was careful not to let her expression give anything away, but learning that Alison had left was a major shock.

'I'll get on with some filing shall I?' she suggested.

'Great. I could do with some sane company while I struggle with this form. The questions they ask would drive a man mad.'

Fiona picked up one of the ring-binder files off the shelf and set about sorting out Rory's paperwork. They worked in silence for several minutes.

After Alison's visit to her room the previous evening, Fiona had had difficulty getting off to sleep. She'd tried to get things straight in her head. Alison had mentioned a row between Ellie and Tim. What had that been about? And why hadn't Ellie mentioned it to Fiona? Had Tim taken off in a bout of fury? And if he had, what exactly had Ellie said to send him over the top?

Then there was Mrs Shaw and the mystery visitor. If it was Tim then he'd discovered where she lived.

By the time Fiona fell into a restless sleep she could still make no sense of anything at all. Alison's early departure was a severe blow. Fiona had been hoping to catch her in Reception and have a quick word with her to update her on her plans. Fiona consoled herself with the knowledge that she did at least have Alison's mobile telephone number and the address of her private flat.

'All done.' Rory flung his pen back into the tray and rubbed his eyes. 'I hope no more guests decide to leave because of all the upheaval.'

'Actually, Rory,' Fiona cleared her throat. 'I'm thinking of leaving.'

'When?' he asked, looking shocked.

'Today, this afternoon. I've had a tip-off about Tim.'

'I see,' Rory said looking at her rather oddly.

'Do you have a problem with that?' Fiona asked wishing Rory didn't look quite so heart-stoppingly handsome. How had she not noticed it before?

Perhaps because this morning was the first time he wasn't scowling at her.

'I do actually.'

'Well, I'm sorry . . . ' Fiona began.

'I'd planned on asking you out to dinner properly this evening, if you're free that is. Sure you wouldn't like to stay on for one more night? I could book us a table at the local bistro.'

Fiona's stomach rumbled at the thought of a decent meal. For the past few days she seemed to have existed on toast and soup. Then she remembered the real reason for her stay at The Hills. She tilted her chin at Rory. 'How can you think about dinner dates when Tim's still missing?'

His smile was dangerously attractive. 'Because I'd far rather ask you out to dinner than discuss your errant brother. But if it makes you feel any better, you can tell me about this tip-off you've received concerning Tim.'

'My next door neighbour said I had a visitor and she mentioned how much he looked like me.'

'And you're going home to check things out?'

'I'm getting nowhere here. I need to speak to Ellie too, my grandmother.'

It still seemed strange to refer to Ellie as her grandmother, but she was her mother's mother and Doreen had only been her grandfather's second wife. Would Tim have been as shocked by this news as Fiona was?

'So you won't stay on for our dinner date tonight?'

Fiona knew it was vitally important not to succumb to his charm. Until she knew more about him, dinner dates with Rory Grainger were off limits.

'I wasn't aware we had one. Honestly, Rory, how can you sit there at your desk calmly filling in your forms when one of your staff has disappeared without a trace and all you can think about is a dinner date? You leave me speechless. What sort of man are you?'

'For someone's who is speechless that was a pretty long speech,' Rory teased Fiona and before she could retaliate he added, 'In answer to your question, I'm a man who would like to apologise for all the inconvenience I've caused you. I did tell the staff not to answer questions about Tim and it seems they have taken me literally, except for Bill who does pretty much as he likes round here.'

Rory held up a hand. 'Let me finish. Most people knew about Tim and Alison. You can't keep something like that quiet around here especially when they are seen together in the pub. I had hoped with Tim out of the way for a while things would cool down. I hadn't really expected Alison Matthews to actually show up again so soon.'

'Why did you invite me to stay,' Fiona demanded, 'if you'd instructed the staff not to answer questions?'

Rory's face crinkled into an embarrassed smile. 'I don't know. Would you believe it if I said love at first sight?'

'Not you as well?'

'As well as who?'

Fiona bit her lip over her second

careless slip of the tongue. She made a gesture of dismissal. 'It was something someone said to me the other day . . . and no, I don't believe in love at first sight. That's for people with stars in their eyes.'

'Who put your stars out, then?' Rory asked gently.

'We need to get something straight,' Fiona began.

Rory leaned forward in his chair. 'Go on,' he urged.

'Somehow I seem to have got involved in looking for a brother who I never knew existed until recently. I thought searching for him might be the distraction I needed after my grandmother's death and my broken engagement.'

Rory drew in a sharp breath. 'I didn't know you were engaged.'

'There's no reason why you should.'

'How long were you engaged for?'

'Eighteen months.'

'Far too long. Gives a man time to change his mind.'

'He did,' Fiona answered in a hollow voice.

Rory made a gesture of annoyance with himself. 'That was thoughtless of me. I'm so sorry for both the remark and your broken engagement.'

'I'm over it now. But at least you can understand my reluctance to even think about another relationship.'

'It's only dinner,' Rory coaxed. 'There'll be no proposal of marriage and I promised I am not otherwise engaged . . . Sorry,' he apologised again, 'couldn't think of another word to use.'

'Darling,' a voice from the doorway interrupted them. 'What's all this talk about being engaged and proposals of marriage?'

A tall slim female with a geometric hair cut strode into Rory's office. She didn't bother glancing at Fiona as she crossed the room and, leaning across Rory's desk, gave him an intimate kiss on the tip of his nose.

'What exactly is going on here?' she asked him.

'Nothing's going on, Issy.' Rory held off from her embrace.

She frowned at him. 'I thought I heard you proposing marriage.'

'Then you heard wrong,' he snapped.

'Good, because I think after our two-year relationship I have first call on any engagement, don't you?' The flinty eyes strayed towards Fiona who was wishing the floor would open and swallow her up. 'Who's this?'

'This is Fiona,' Fiona said in reply, annoyed that this girl, whoever she was, should speak about her as if she weren't there! 'Who are you?'

'Fiona, meet Issy Barlow,' Rory introduced them.

'I'm also the long-term partner of Rory Grainger,' Issy added, 'so if you've got any ideas in that direction, you can forget about them.'

Fiona looked from Issy to Rory, then back to a triumphant Issy. The look on Rory's face was enough to convince Fiona Issy was telling the truth.

'I have no ideas of anything at all,'

Fiona said quietly.

'I'm pleased to hear it.' Issy's cheekbones moved in a parody of a smile as she turned back to Rory. 'I raced down here when I heard on breakfast news that the dreaded Alison Matthews had checked herself in. I didn't want her getting her claws into you, darling, now that Tim Dalrymple isn't here to distract her. I thought we'd done with all this nuisance of office staff chatting you up after I persuaded your last personal assistant that her attentions were unwelcome. I soon packed her off to Australia.'

'Fiona is not office staff,' Rory began.

'I have such a lot to tell you, darling,' Issy ignored his comment about Fiona, 'about my new modelling contract. It's very high profile, mega media coverage and there's talk about it leading to a part in a film.'

'I'm very pleased for you, Issy,' Rory answered with a wooden expression on his face. 'Now I've got a lot to do.'

Issy pouted at him. 'A teensy bit

more enthusiasm would be nice, darling. I know, shall we go and have a drink to celebrate? I am absolutely exhausted.' She stifled a delicate yawn. 'Early morning shoots are a killer to social life. Still when I'm living here I shall have an army of staff to look after me, won't I?'

'You've done your worst, Issy, now please leave.' Rory's voice was colder than Fiona had ever heard it before.

'Darling, surely you're not going to escort me off the premises? Now about tonight — shall we go out to dinner or would you prefer we had something more intimate on a tray in our room? I've discovered this divine new Thai place down by the river. We could phone up for an order. They do food to go.'

'I may not be here when you get back,' Fiona called after Issy and Rory as they made their way out of the office.

'Fiona,' Rory began, turning in the doorway.

'Rory,' Paula called from the reception desk, 'can I have a quick word?'

'Coming.' Issy seized her chance to hustle Rory out of the office.

Fiona had a wild urge to fling the rest of Rory's filing in the air. She had been right about him all along. She was better off without men, she decided, as she threw the last file back onto the shelf. It landed with a satisfying thud. More fool her for falling for Rory's chat- up lines and the soft brown eyes.

Fiona snatched up her bag. On her way back to Rose Cottage she'd call in on Ellie Marsden. She didn't care whether Frank was playing golf or not. Ellie Marsden knew a whole lot more about this affair than she was letting on and Fiona wasn't about to go easy on her. She was fed up with people lying to her. It was time somebody started telling the truth.

Rory's telephone burst into life as Fiona yanked open Rory's office door. She decided to let it ring, but then took pity on the girls on the desk. They were being besieged by several new arrivals. Fiona hesitated, a wicked smile curving her lips. If by any chance it was the press on the line she could always do the dirty on Rory and tell them all about Alison. Shaking her head knowing nothing would make her behave quite that badly she lifted the receiver.

'Is Rory there?' A voice asked.

''Fraid not.'

'Right.' The caller hesitated. 'Well, could you tell him I've made headway in my investigations?'

'Headway in your investigations,' Fiona repeated as she wrote it down on a notepad. 'Will he know what that means?' she asked in puzzlement.

'I've been looking at the electoral roll and I found this address — Rose Cottage in a place called Grange Heath. I called round there, but no one was in. Some nosy neighbour said she had Doreen's telephone number and would get in touch with her for me, at least I think that's what she said. She wasn't making an awful lot of sense. She kept looking at me as though I'd fallen out of a tree,' the caller told her in a big rush. 'Anyway — hello, are you still there?'

'Yes, I'm here.'

'Thought we'd been cut off. I heard a funny noise on the line.'

'I'm still here,' Fiona replied in a faint voice.

'Good, did you get all that? Tell Rory I should be back at work by Sunday at the latest and that I'm really grateful he gave me time off to do all this. It's all been such a shock.'

'You didn't give me your name,' Fiona spoke carefully. After so many misunderstandings she wanted to be absolutely sure who she was talking to.

'Sorry, you must be new,' he laughed lightly, 'should have introduced myself properly. My name is Tim Dalrymple.'

★ ★ ★

'What do you think, Jim?'

Mrs Shaw's husband didn't look up from his catalogue. 'Whatever you say, love,' he replied, evading a direct reply.

'You know me, I'm not a gossip and Doreen did tell me in confidence.'

'Yes.' His eyes still did not stray from the page in front of him.

'I knew Fiona was keeping something back from me. I've known her since she was a little girl and I could always tell if she was fibbing and I don't think she's gone on holiday at all. I think whatever she's up to it's something to do with Angus's first wife and this young man who called the day before yesterday.'

Jim held his cup out for more tea. Mrs Shaw picked up the pot distractedly.

'They should have told her. I know it's none of my business but it's not right is it?' she said as she absentmindedly poured his tea.

'No, it's not,' Jim agreed, sipped his tea.

'Poor little mite. You should have seen her the night she arrived. November it was. I can still remember it to this day. The wind was howling around and bits of trees were flying about all over the place. I was out walking Mitzi, you remember her? She was a sweet little dog wasn't she? Anyway out of the darkness this woman appears from nowhere with a bundle in her arms. Gave me such a fright. Of course I never knew what Ellie looked like. She'd already disappeared off the scene by the time I met Doreen but she told me all about her and Gillian later.'

'Course she did.' Jim finished his tea. 'Well, I'll be off now,' he said.

'So if this young man comes calling again, do you think I should tell him?'

'It's up to you, love,' Jim replied, shrugging on his tweed jacket. 'I'll just be up at the allotment.'

'Don't forget your sandwiches,' Mrs Shaw called after her husband as he made a hasty exit before his wife could involve him in any more of the unfolding drama next door.

The kitchen was quiet after he had left. Mrs Shaw cupped her chin in her hand. Nobody thought anything about that sort of thing these days and times were different now, but over twenty years ago it would have caused such a scandal. People talked and, in a village like this, what they didn't know they made up. She didn't blame Doreen for keeping quiet. In her position, Mrs Shaw would have done exactly the same — it was nobody's business but her own.

Her lips tightened. It was that Angus Weir's fault. The number of times Mrs Shaw had heard him and Doreen arguing about the constant stream of females coming and going at the house. Clients, he called them. How come his clients were mostly female? A reluctant smile softened her lips. The trouble was he was such a charming man, always raised his hat and opened doors for the ladies, and he knew how to deliver a compliment. He always noticed when she'd had her hair done or was wearing a new dress — something Jim never did.

Although he and Doreen frequently argued she wouldn't hear a word against him either and none of it affected Fiona. She had been a bright little child, always top of the class at school. She was well cared for and happy and there was no denying old Angus doted on the girl. Nothing was too much trouble for his little princess. Extra dancing lessons, swimming, drama club, he was always driving her and her friends everywhere in that huge old-fashioned car of his and every summer they gave a wonderful party for her in the garden with a magician and balloons and a barbecue.

It had been a perfect time and that was why Mrs Shaw was reluctant to destroy the memories Fiona would hold of her childhood.

She had expected Fiona to call back after that message she left on her mobile. Mrs Shaw shook her head. Perhaps it was better to do nothing. If her suspicions about the caller were wrong then she would have stirred up a hornet's nest and all for nothing. Jim was right. Whatever Angus Weir got up to in his private life, it was none of their business.

★ ★ ★

As far as Fiona was concerned, if she never saw The Hills or Rory Grainger again it would be too soon. For a little while she had actually believed him when he said he didn't mix business with pleasure and that was why he always went out on his nights off. She knew better now.

The staff would have known about his relationship with Issy Barlow and that he had taken Fiona out for a drink. Someone had probably told Issy and that was why she'd appeared out of the blue that morning.

Fiona had caught the sympathetic looks cast in her direction as she hurried out of Rory's office. She couldn't wait to shake the dust of The Hills off her feet.

Her hatchback bumped along the back road leading from The Hill's staff entrance towards the main road. How many days ago was it when she had first met Rory on this very road? She slowed up in order to avoid a large pothole. She must not think about him. Not only had he lied about Issy, he had lied about Tim. He'd known all along where Tim was. Tim hadn't gone missing at all. Rory had given him authorised leave of absence and from what Tim had said during their brief conversation, it sounded as though he had kept Rory fully updated.

Tim had rung off so quickly Fiona hadn't had time to tell him who she was. She had dialled one-four-seven-one to trace the call, but the caller number had been withheld. For a while she had stood by the telephone unable to move, her heart beating quicker than a trip hammer.

She had actually spoken to Tim, her brother. She was glad Rory's desk was such a solid affair. If it hadn't been she doubted her legs would have supported her. Sinking into Rory's leather chair she took several deep breaths. Tim was looking for her. It would do no good staying on at The Hills. She had to get home as soon as possible.

Fiona couldn't think straight as she drove. Where would Tim be heading now? Would he go back to Rose Cottage? There hadn't been time to return Mrs Shaw's call. Then there was Ellie Marsden. Fiona desperately needed to have a word with her too.

Alison Matthews had mentioned an argument between Tim and Ellie, yet Ellie had made no mention of it. Had it been about Fiona? With a decided twist of her steering wheel, Fiona turned her car towards April Cottage. It wasn't fair to involve Mrs Shaw in any of this. Ellie was the woman who had all the answers.

'Darling.' Ellie's face lit up as she answered the door. She was dressed in her usual cashmere and tailored skirt. 'How lovely to see you. Come in. You're just in time for tea. I'm all on my own so we won't be interrupted.'

Fiona followed Ellie through to the lounge. Racing was on the television. Fiona caught a glimpse of the jockeys' bright silks before Ellie switched it off.

'I love to watch it,' she smiled. 'Angus was a great one for the horses and when Frank and I were in Hong Kong we followed it avidly. Golf has never been my thing, so while Frank plays I watch the horse racing. I like an occasional flutter on Derby Day and the National. Angus started my interest in horses, I suppose.' She flushed and again Fiona got the impression that Angus and not Frank Marsden had been the love of Ellie's life.

'But you haven't come here to listen to me rambling on about the old days.' Ellie recollected herself. 'Have you heard from Tim?'

'Yes. He phoned The Hills this morning. I was in Rory's Grainger's office and I just happened to take the call.'

Fiona perched awkwardly on the elegant French chair opposite Ellie. It looked so delicate she was scared it would simply snap like a twig under her weight.

Ellie's face actually lit up. 'Oh, thank goodness for that! And is he all right?'

'I think so. He didn't actually realise who I was. He was calling Rory to say he would be back at work shortly.'

'Why hasn't he been in touch? Why did he disappear without a word?'

'I think you know the answer to those questions.'

'I don't know what you mean,' Ellie replied looking flustered.

'Then I'll spell it out to you. You and Tim had an argument. What exactly was it about?' Fiona demanded.

She watched Ellie's face turn deep pink.

'An argument?' she blustered.

'Ellie, it is time you told me the truth. You've kept things hidden from Tim and me for far too long. We have a right to know.'

Ellie licked her lips, then dabbed at them with a delicate lace handkerchief.

'We had words, yes,' Ellie admitted, 'and Tim was upset, but that was no reason not to contact me.'

'You still haven't answered my question.'

Ellie picked an imaginary piece of fluff off her jumper. She blinked hard then, as if coming to a major and difficult decision, she raised her head and looked Fiona in the eye.

'I hadn't seen or heard from Doreen in years. We didn't really get on. I had already broken up with Angus before he met her, but I suppose in my heart of hearts I always wanted him to come back to me. Once he got together with Doreen I knew that was impossible. In a way I blamed her for what happened, although it wasn't her fault. When I read her obituary in the local paper and realised she was still living not ten miles away from me I was so shocked. I realised I had wasted so much time being bitter and that I was no more than a silly old woman, nursing a hurt that never should have existed in the first place.'

Fiona felt her first pang of sympathy. Ellie Marsden's pride had cost her dear.

'Doreen would have understood,' Fiona said softly.

'Would she?' Ellie asked with a look of hope.

'She was the most non-judgemental person I know, although some of the light went out of her life when Angus died.'

'Mine too.'

There was the suggestion of a tear in Ellie's eye as she gave a watery smile.

'He was such a rogue, but we all loved him.'

'You haven't told me about Tim,' Fiona urged before Ellie lost her courage.

Ellie swallowed hard. 'I wrote to the funeral directors because I wasn't sure of Doreen's exact address. I thought perhaps she might have moved from Rose Cottage after Angus died. I was hoping you still lived with her because I decided, no matter what Frank said, it was time you and Tim knew the truth. After I posted my letter I confessed to Tim what I'd done.'

Ellie stalled to a halt again.

'Please, I have to know.' Fiona touched Ellie's hand. Despite the warmth of the day, her skin was cold.

Ellie coughed, then blew her nose. 'As you know Tim wasn't aware you were living with Doreen.'

'He wasn't aware of me at all, because you told him that I was . . . ' Fiona said.

'I realise that was wrong of me,' Ellie interrupted, 'and that I shouldn't have let things go on for so long, but the time was never right to tell Tim the truth. He was away at school and then university and suddenly he was a grown man with a life of his own. What was I supposed to do?'

'It must have been such a shock for him to discover I was alive.'

Ellie lowered her eyes. 'He said some harsh things to me, about how he used to cry himself to sleep at boarding school because he missed you so much. I've never seen him so angry. He's normally such a placid person.' Ellie was now sobbing openly, 'Fiona, I am so sorry. If only I'd known how badly I hurt him. I've been out of my mind with worry after he drove off. The security guards said he hardly waited for them to open the gates before he raced through them. No one's seen or heard from him since. He hasn't done anything silly has he? Please tell me hasn't. I would never forgive myself if he did. It's all my fault.'

The stricken expression on Ellie's face softened Fiona's anger. She didn't doubt Ellie had acted as she thought best at the time. She also didn't doubt that her husband Frank had probably influenced her. He sounded the sort of man who would not welcome his wife's grandchildren into his life. They would probably disrupt his social schedule and take her away from him.

'As far as I know he's fine. He seems to have found out about Doreen.'

'Found out what about her?' Ellie's face was now as pale as a carnival mask.

'My neighbour, Mrs Shaw, said a man called at Rose Cottage the day before yesterday looking for her. I think it was Tim.'

'I didn't get the chance to tell him Doreen had died. He stormed out of the house after I told him about you.'

'Is there anything else you haven't told me? Because if there isn't I should get back to Rose Cottage in case he calls again. Are there any more skeletons in the family cupboard I should know about?'

There was the sound of a door being opened and voices in the kitchen.

'Frank's back.' Ellie stood up. 'I expect he's brought his golfing partners with him. They often come back for drinks.'

She hurried to the mirror and began repairing her hair and make-up.

'Goodness, I look a mess.' She scrubbed at the tearstains on her face with her damp tissue.

'I'd better be on my way.' Fiona picked up her bag.

Ellie did not insist she stay and meet Frank and from the way Fiona was feeling at the moment, she didn't think she wanted to be introduced to him ever.

'Find Tim for me, darling,' Ellie pleaded, turning away from the mirror. 'Then I'll tell you both everything together. You'll probably never speak to me again, but it's no more than I deserve.'

Ellie looked so stricken, Fiona had no hesitation in hugging her. She wasn't plump like Doreen, she was bony and frail, but Doreen had always insisted there was nothing a hug couldn't cure.

'That's silly talk,' Fiona chided her. 'If Tim's half the man you say he is, he'll understand. He's in a state of shock, that's all. I'll find him for you and drag him back here by his coat tails. How's that? Do we have a deal?' Fiona said kindly.

'A deal.' Ellie nodded. 'I know I don't

deserve it but can you ever find it in your heart to forgive me?'

'There's nothing to forgive. I had a lovely childhood. Tim was happy with you. We're all going to meet up again. You know, after Doreen died I thought I had no one in the world, and yet now I find I've got a grandmother and a brother and it's a lovely feeling.'

'Bless you,' Ellie stroked Fiona's cheek. 'I've got lots of Gillian's things to show you. We'll do a bit of feminine bonding once we've found that wretched grandson of mine and taken him to task for disappearing without a word.'

'It's a date.'

Before Fiona drove away from April Cottage she checked her texts. There was one from Alison: *Can U come? At flat with Tim.*

Fiona's fingers trembled. She could barely tap in her reply: *Coming now.* Then she remembered Ellie. She ought to tell her. Fiona opened the car door then hesitated before closing it again.

Ellie had waited so long for this moment Fiona decided she could wait a little longer. Turning the key, she started her car and headed back towards Alison's studio flat.

8

Fiona hated driving in London. There was nowhere to park near Alison's studio flat and she drove around for a quarter of an hour before she spotted a space that she could just squeeze her car into.

Late lunchtime shoppers were ambling along the pavements and several young mothers with buggies were emerging from a playgroup. It was impossible to rush and despite Fiona's protests that she was in a hurry, no one really moved out of her way. Fuming behind a community dog walker who seemed to be exercising more than the numbers of dogs officially allowed, Fiona tried to make sense of all that was going on in her head.

Tim and Alison seemed to be reconciled. Had Alison told him about their meeting at The Hills? And how much did Rory know about all this?

Fiona chewed her lip, ignoring the surge of emotion that went through her body whenever she remembered Rory. She had begun to think he was different from George Ross, but it seemed her first assessment of red-haired men was accurate. They weren't to be trusted. She pitied Issy, Rory's girlfriend, if every time they were apart, Rory made a play for another female.

Fiona eventually managed to struggle by the dog walker without entangling her legs in the half dozen or so leads that were causing havoc to other pedestrians as well as herself. In all the confusion she had lost her bearings, but she didn't want to stop walking in case the dog walker overtook her again.

Alison had intimated that the studio was her bolthole from the press so Fiona didn't want to ask anyone for directions. She snatched a quick glance at the address she had scribbled down on her piece of paper. Alison had told her it was down by the canal off a small side street.

She spied a passageway that indicated a lead down to the water and she quickly turned down the gloomy short cut.

Fiona shivered from the loss of sunlight as the buildings either side of the passageway loomed over her. Her shoes slipped on the damp, slimy cobblestones and she wrinkled her nose against the dank odour of rotten fruit.

In the distance she could near noises from the river. At least she was going in the right direction she thought as she stumbled on.

She could hardly believe that Tim, her brother was waiting for her in his girlfriend's flat. If this were a movie they would have got together somewhere scenic with a full forty-piece orchestra doing its stuff in the background. Instead she was shivering and slipping her way down a decidedly dodgy back street that didn't look like it lead anywhere at all.

Her breath came in short sharp bursts as she battled on through the discarded orange peel and empty fast food cartons that littered the gutter. She banged her knee on a bollard as panic began to grip her and then behind some railings she spied a small set of steps. She clattered down them and emerged into a small courtyard bathed in sunlight and there opposite her was the address she was looking for.

She ran across the road, earning a loud blast from a passing motorist. She waved an apology and before she could have second thoughts pressed the bell for Alison's flat.

★ ★ ★

The moment she saw Tim she knew he was her brother. Even though she had only been a baby when they were separated she would have recognised him anywhere. He was so like their grandfather Angus Weir. They both possessed the same welcoming smile and Tim's impulsive gesture of enveloping Fiona in a bear hug after he had answered the door was exactly what Angus would have done. Angus didn't stint on hugs and neither did Tim.

'My little sister!' Tim's voice was hoarse as he crushed her ribs then held her at arm's length and studied her face. 'I told you she was beautiful, Jean, didn't I?' he asked, his face a picture of joy as he jostled Fiona back into Alison's lounge. 'I meant Al . . . I've got to stop calling her Jean — it confuses people.'

Alison who'd stood apart from the reunion was dragged into the circle as Tim put his arm around her. Her voice was soft as she smiled at the pair of them. 'Hello, Fiona. Lovely to see you again.'

Fiona tried to speak but the words caught in her throat.

'I owe it all to Al, you know,' Tim went on. 'If I hadn't met her she wouldn't have started me on this family history thing. Isn't she the most amazing girl you've ever met?'

'Moments ago,' Fiona managed to

find her voice, 'I thought I was!'

It seemed so easy to lapse into a comfortable relationship with Tim. It was as if she had her grandfather back again and until today Fiona hadn't realised how much she missed him.

'I didn't mean . . . ' Tim began, then his eyes crinkled at the corners. 'You're teasing me, aren't you?'

'We ought to celebrate,' Alison announced, 'I'll pop out for a bottle of champagne and leave you two to get to know each other in private, shall I? Where's my disguise?'

Fiona burst out laughing as Alison reappeared minutes later wearing a bright red beret over a dark wig, and quite the most dreadful sunglasses she had ever seen in her life.

'Works a treat,' Alison said, adopting a stooping pose and speaking in a croaky voice, 'Bye guys. Won't be long.'

Neither Tim nor Fiona spoke for a few moments after she'd left.

'You've got sandy hair,' Fiona spoke first. Somehow she had expected Tim to have darker hair like her own.

'And I burn up in the sun,' Tim said, 'that's why Al and I are going somewhere cool for our honeymoon.'

'What?' Fiona demanded, forgetting all about her aversion to men with reddish coloured hair.

Tim made a face. 'Sorry. State secret. We're engaged but I'm calling on the family honour here, Sis, not to tell a soul.'

'I won't, but,' Fiona put a hand to her head trying to unravel the knot of confusion inside, 'I thought that as well as walking out on Rory Grainger, you had walked out on Alison.'

'I didn't walk out on either of them.'

'That's not how Rory's telling it.'

'I recognise your voice.' Tim's eyes widened. 'It was you who answered the telephone at The Hills, wasn't it?'

'Yes, but you rang off before I could tell you who I was.'

'I thought you were Rory's new assistant. Issy managed to scare the last one off to Australia.'

'Was it you who called on Mrs Shaw?' Fiona demanded. She had no wish to hear about Rory or Issy Barlow.

'Look, let's calm down a bit and start at the beginning. I'll go first shall I?' Tim suggested.

'I don't know where to start.' Fiona still couldn't stop smiling at Tim. To see him here in the flesh was better than all her birthdays rolled together.

'Sit down,' Tim urged her. 'I'm afraid there isn't much room. Al's the untidiest person on the planet.' He gave another soppy grin. 'Don't you think she's the most wonderful person in the world?'

'She feels the same way about you,' Fiona said.

'No kidding? You know the first time we met . . .'

'Look, Tim,' Fiona dragged him down onto the sofa next to her, 'I promise to talk about Alison as much as you like later, but not now. There's loads of other stuff to get through first.'

Tim blinked his sandy eyelashes at

her. 'You're right. Sorry. Still can't believe anyone as fantastic as Al would want to get engaged to a geek like me.'

'You're not a geek,' Fiona protested, 'well . . . maybe a bit,' she grinned as he donned a huge pair of tortoiseshell glasses.

'I took them off to propose, but I'm not very good at seeing without them,' he explained. 'That's better. Hey, you really are beautiful. How come you got all the good-looking genes in the family?'

'Tim,' Fiona put her hand in his, 'I'm all the family you've got, apart from Ellie. Doreen, Angus's second wife, the woman I thought was my grandmother, died just over a month ago.'

'I guessed as much,' Tim confessed.

'You did? How? I mean you didn't even know she existed.'

'It's a long story but after I'd calmed down a bit on learning you were still alive, I wondered what had prompted Ellie to tell me about you after so long.'

'Go on,' Fiona encouraged.

'Despite everything Ellie and Frank had told me when I was a child, I sensed you were alive. I don't know why but I did. We were so close you see. You won't remember but everyone used to laugh at me because I was so proud of having a baby sister. Then you weren't there any more and it was horrible. My whole life changed . . . ' His voice croaked with emotion. 'Sorry.' Tim's lips struggled into a smile. 'Not very manly is it?'

'It's all right.' Fiona squeezed his fingers. 'I'm here now and I'm not going anywhere ever again. Can I be a bridesmaid?' She nudged him in an attempt to cheer him up.

'Swore you to silence, Sis!' he protested.

'Sorry, forgot!' Her ruse worked and Tim's cheerful smile was back. 'Now, where was I?'

'Arguing with Ellie?'

'Right. I needed to get away from April Cottage for a while and The Hills as well after this thing with Al blew up.

I had so much going on in my mind, so when Rory suggested I might like to take some leave owing to me I went for it. I told him I had some personal stuff to sort out and he was fine about it.'

'But why on earth didn't you contact Ellie all this time?' Fiona demanded. 'Didn't you realise that she's been simply out of her mind with worry?'

Tim looked down at the floor. 'I'm not proud of myself on that one, Sis, but I wanted her to know how it felt to lose someone you love. Frank lied to me about you and she let him get away with it.'

'You must contact her,' Fiona insisted, 'no matter what she's done.'

'I will, very soon. I promise.'

'So where have you been all this time that I've been looking for you?'

'With an old school friend. He works in the public records office and he looked up your birth certificate for me. I knew you were three years younger than me and as I'd been born in Dorking, I guessed you were born there as well. I tried to find Angus's details because I knew Frank wasn't my real grandfather but I wasn't successful.'

'So then what did you do?'

'I went back to basics. Ellie reads the local newspaper from cover to cover so I got some back copies and I found an obituary for a Doreen Weir, widow of Angus. It said beloved grandmother, but it didn't give any details, although I put two and two together.'

'So that's how you knew Doreen was dead?'

'I wasn't sure of anything. It's not that an unusual a name. I found Doreen's address from the census returns but before I barged in on a totally innocent person and caused havoc I had to be sure she was the Doreen Weir who had been married to our grandfather. So I went calling on Rose Cottage.'

'That was when you met Mrs Shaw?'

'Is that your next door neighbour?'

'Yes.'

'She's a canny old bird isn't she?

Wouldn't give anything away.'

'She's fiercely protective of me but once you get to know her you'll like her.'

'If she's as loyal to me as she is to you, then I know I will.'

'I can't believe I was away looking for you at the same time you were knocking on the door of Rose Cottage.'

'Al says Rory let you stay in my room.'

'He said I could.' Fiona hesitated, uncertain how to go on.

'Sis?' Tim picked up the expression on her face. 'Is something wrong? You have to tell me what it is.'

'Rory Grainger . . . ' she admitted.

'He's the best isn't he? Like your Mrs Shaw he's very loyal. He hasn't had an easy life and I suppose compared to him I've been pampered but he doesn't hold that against me.'

'Did Rory know where you were?' Fiona asked.

'Sort of. He didn't actually know my friend's address but he knew how to contact me. I had my mobile and I kept him updated.'

'Then why did he pretend he didn't know anything about where you'd gone?'

'I think I know the answer to that. He had this girlfriend called Issy.'

'I've met her,' Fiona said.

'Have you?' Tim looked surprised. 'I thought she was off the scene. Anyway, she sold a story to the press about a guest who was staying at The Hills. Rory went ballistic and now he doesn't trust anyone he doesn't know.'

Despite her antipathy Fiona could understand how Rory felt. She supposed he'd had no reason to trust her. She had bowled up out of the blue, claiming to be Tim's sister and to the best of Rory's knowledge, Tim didn't have a sister. His attitude had only changed when Fiona had produced the letter of introduction that Ellie had given her.

'He might have thought you'd stumbled on a story about Al and me,'

Tim said, 'Issy could have known about it and been up to her old tricks, getting you in to The Hills as some sort of under cover agent. She's always short of money and journalists can be generous if they sense a good story. Al's hot news and if they found out about her and me,' Tim shrugged, 'it would be enough to make anyone go into hiding.'

'We didn't get off to a very good start — Rory and me,' Fiona admitted, 'and then Issy reappeared on the scene just as I was getting to know him.'

Tim frowned. 'He told me under no circumstances was she to be let back in. Trouble is, there's no keeping Issy out.'

'They seemed pretty much like an item to me.'

'No way! That's long over,' Tim said firmly. 'Do you like him then, Sis? Rory?' he asked with a wry brotherly grin.

Fiona coloured up. 'Let's not waste time talking about him.'

'I'll take that as a yes, then, shall I?'

Fiona ignored the gibe. 'So, what do

we do now?' she asked.

'We have some champagne!' Alison burst through the door brandishing a bottle and creating a welcome interruption. 'Have I stayed away long enough? Did you talk things through? Came back a bit earlier than I intended because I thought I caught sight of a familiar face lurking about downstairs.'

'I'll get some glasses.'

Tim disappeared into the kitchen. Alison whipped off her wig.

'This thing itches so much it gives me hives,' she complained.

'Know I'm not supposed to know,' Fiona whispered, as Alison ran her fingers through her hair, 'but congratulations. I'm to be bridesmaid by the way!'

'Brilliant! You'll love my sister — she'll have to be one too. The Smiths are very hot on family and now I've got a lovely new sister, life couldn't be better.'

Tim came back with some glasses and plonked them on the table then began undoing the champagne cork.

'Darling,' Alison beamed at him as the cork popped, 'you'll never guess who I saw outside.'

'No, who?' he asked, battling with the bubbles as they began to run down the side of the bottle.

Alison paused for effect then said, 'Rory Grainger.'

9

Fiona tossed her head in challenge as Rory strode into Alison's studio flat. His eyes flared at the sight of her sitting on Alison's sofa. 'What are you doing here?' he demanded.

'Visiting my brother,' she retorted.

'I don't believe you,' Rory replied.

'Tim,' Fiona turned to him, 'perhaps you'd like to convince Rory that we really are brother and sister. He seems to think I'm a reporter trying to get an exclusive out of your relationship with Alison.'

'You don't really believe that do you, Rory?' Tim said in disbelief.

'Ellie had to give me a letter of introduction before he would take me at my word,' Fiona crowed, looking back at Rory whose expression was a mixture of embarrassment and confusion.

'That was because . . . ' Rory began.

'I'm not interested in any more of your stories,' Fiona cut him off.

'Steady on, Sis,' Tim tried to calm her down. 'None of this is Rory's fault.'

'Isn't it? In that case why did he tell me he had no idea where you were when he knew all along?'

'I didn't know — exactly,' Rory said.

'But you did give Tim leave of absence from work.'

'He's right, Sis. I told you he didn't know.'

'Is this a private argument or can anyone join in?' Alison's amused voice broke into the interchange between Rory, Fiona and Tim. 'Honestly, Fiona, do you and Rory always bicker like an old married couple?'

'Sorry, Alison.' Fiona flushed, wishing Alison had chosen a better comparison. 'I didn't mean to drag you into all this.'

'I think I've already been dragged in. If it hadn't been for me, Timmy wouldn't have taken off . . . and don't worry, Timmy and I shout at each other

162

all the time, don't we, darling?'

Tim went red behind his spectacles. 'Not *all* the time,' he protested.

'Stop teasing him, Alison,' Fiona chided her, taking pity on Tim's discomfort.

'I keep forgetting you're his little sister, Fiona. I'll have to watch what I say with you around if I don't want you jumping down my neck. Isn't it terrific news, Rory? They've found each other again after all these years? It'll make a wonderful story when we officially announce our engagement.'

'Your what?' Rory snapped his attention from Fiona to Alison.

'Honestly,' Fiona protested, 'you two had better make it official as soon as possible before the whole world gets to know about it.'

'I'll get onto my agent first thing,' Alison promised. 'Actually,' she added as if she had just noticed, 'Fiona has a point, Rory — what *are* you doing here?'

'I came to see if Tim was with you.'

'Why?' Tim asked.

'Your grandmother is getting desperate for news of you.'

'You could have left a message on my mobile.'

'I also came to warn Alison that Issy is on her case.'

'Issy Barlow?' Alison exploded. 'Don't tell me she's back! I thought you'd managed to get rid of her.'

'So did I,' Rory said through gritted teeth. 'She turned up yesterday out of the blue because she'd heard you were booked in at The Hills.'

Alison raised her eyes in exasperation. 'That woman's got a radar system second to none. We were at drama school together,' she explained to Fiona. 'She's forever playing the old friend card in the hope that I'll be able to get her a part on television.'

'And she's got contacts in the newspaper world,' Tim put in with feeling. 'They tailed me for a while because she tipped them off about a possible story.'

'Well, thanks for the warning, Rory,' Alison said. 'I'm sorry you've had such a long drive up from Surrey. What say we all go out as a foursome for dinner? We've all got loads to talk about.'

'I would actually like a quiet word with Fiona,' Rory said in a voice that made her feel uncomfortable.

'Me?' Fiona asked startled.

'I thought Tim might know where you were if he'd been successful in tracking you down. I didn't realise you'd actually be here with him.'

'Before you start accusing me of going through your private records, I think I ought to tell you that Alison who gave me her private address herself. She came looking for Tim that night she was at The Hills.'

'That's right. I escaped out the sauna fire exit,' Alison explained, 'and crept up the back stairs to the staff quarters. I got the shock of my life when Fiona answered Timmy's door. You didn't really think she was working for the press, did you, Rory?'

'Look, er,' Tim began sidling towards the door, 'why don't you put your disguise back on, Al?'

'Why?' Alison demanded.

'I thought perhaps we could go out for that meal, just you and me? Leave Rory and Fiona to it here?'

Alison's brow cleared. 'Yes, of course. Good idea, Timmy. Where's my wig. You two don't want an old engaged couple cramping your style, do you?'

'No, you don't have to leave,' Fiona began, 'I'd like to . . . '

'Here.' Tim crammed Alison's wig onto her head and pushed a giggling Alison out of the door before Fiona could finish what she had been going to say.

'Catch up with you later, Sis,' he called over his shoulder, 'and don't let Rory give you any grief.'

'I've got to go too.' Fiona stood up.

'Not before I've had my say,' Rory said quietly. 'Please?'

With her heartbeat drumming in her ears, Fiona sat back down again as the door closed behind Tim and Alison.

'I want to explain,' he began.

'What about?'

'Amongst other things, Issy . . . '

'There's no need. I don't want to listen to any more of your explanations.'

The truth was Fiona didn't want to start believing in Rory, or deciding that, when they weren't arguing, she quite liked him. Life was a whole lot easier to deal with when Rory Grainger was not being nice to her and right now her life was full enough without further complications.

'Do you remember the day we first met by the staff entrance to The Hills?'

'I could hardly forget it, could I?' Fiona protested with a wry smile to her lips.

'I'd just come from visiting Issy.'

'Well, thank you for letting me know that . . . '

'We'd had a scene. I was still fired up and I suppose I took some of my anger out on you. I'd told Issy things were finally over between us and she didn't take the news very well.'

'That was hardly my fault.'

'I know,' Rory admitted. 'But I was so annoyed about the publicity story she'd leaked to the press. Then when I bumped into you hovering by the staff entrance and asking questions about Tim what was I supposed to think?'

'You could have given me a chance to explain.'

'I'll admit I jumped to the wrong conclusion, but you didn't seem to know anything about him, not even what he really looked like, and . . . ' Rory's tired eyes smiled at her, 'I'd had enough. I knew the bosses would tear me to shreds over the Alison Matthews affair. I didn't want any more trouble.'

'You could have sent me on my way without letting me in and then giving me Tim's room to use.'

'I know but after you showed me the letter from Ellie Marsden I realised I'd made a mistake about you. I knew Tim had a few personal problems to sort out and I wondered if they were anything to do with you. Quite without realising it, I seemed to have got caught up in them. By having you at The Hills, it sort of eased things for me. Bill was being a bit of a nuisance too before you came onto the scene and I wasn't finding it easy fobbing him off, but once you arrived, he left me alone. Mrs Marsden also stopped ringing me every hour on the hour which was a great relief.'

Rory gave a shamefaced smile. 'Your filing skills were the icing on the cake.'

'So that's all I am,' Fiona retaliated, 'a trouble shooting go-between who happens to be good at filing? Well, thanks a bunch.'

'That's not what I meant,' Rory spoke through gritted teeth. 'If you must know I simply couldn't think of another good excuse to keep you at The Hills unless I just pretended not to know anything at all about Tim's whereabouts.'

'We're going round in circles, Rory. First you didn't want me there, then . . .'

'I've already explained about that.'

' . . . then you're inventing excuses to virtually keep me under house arrest.' Fiona warmed to her theme. 'And all the while you have a girlfriend lurking around in the background.'

'Issy is not my girlfriend any more, I told you that!'

'She still seems to think she is and until you've cleared things up with her any relationship between us is a non-starter! And now I really do have to go.'

'Fiona . . .' Rory put out a hand to detain her.

'No, Rory.' She shook him off. 'I mean it. You thought I was a member of the press and you didn't trust me. Fine. I've got a history with red headed men and I have reason not to trust them.'

She picked up her handbag.

'I expect Tim will be back at work soon and he says he's going to contact

Ellie as soon as possible, so that leaves our relationship at an end, doesn't it?'

Before Rory could stop her, Fiona yanked open Alison's door and ran down the stairs into the street outside.

10

Fiona inhaled the smell of damp earth as she watered her beans. It always had the power to soothe her. In the distance she could hear the drone of a lawn-mower. The evening air was cool and fresh against her skin after the heat and dirt of the drive home from London.

'Hello, dear.' Mrs Shaw poked her head over the hedge. 'I see you're back.'

'I was going to call round in the morning,' Fiona stifled a sigh.

Much as she genuinely liked Mrs Shaw and appreciated everything her neighbour had done for her, this evening she really needed to be on her own.

'Of course.' Mrs Shaw smiled brightly. 'How are you?'

Fiona put down her watering can. It was never easy fobbing her off.

'Have you time for a cup of tea?'

Fiona's manners kicked in because she knew she was being ungrateful. Mrs Shaw had looked after her cottage while she'd been away after all.

'The thing is,' Mrs Shaw began, not immediately taking up Fiona's offer, 'I was wondering if by any chance you had Ellie Marsden's telephone number?'

'Ellie Marsden? You want to speak to her?' Fiona frowned.

Even though the light was going from the day Fiona could see Mrs Shaw was having difficulty containing her agitation.

'Actually I do. I've got something on my mind and I really would like to talk to her about it. You don't mind do you?'

'No,' Fiona said, 'you'd better come round while I find it.'

Mrs Shaw was on her front doorstep in a flash. 'I won't stay for tea, dear,' she said as Fiona passed over the number, 'I can see you're tired after your little break. We'll talk when you've had a chance to settle in.'

'Are you sure you're all right?' Fiona

173

asked in concern. It was most unlike Mrs Shaw to turn down the offer of a cup of tea.

'I'm fine, dear, and I'm so pleased you're back safely. We'll catch up later.'

'Yes,' Fiona echoed faintly, surprised at the swiftness of Mrs Shaw's exit.

Shaking her head in perplexity, she went back outside to turn off the water and lock up the shed for the night. She was feeling far too tired to think anything through. If Mrs Shaw wanted to play cloak and dagger with Ellie Marsden then Fiona was prepared to go along with it, although what her next-door neighbour could have to say to her grandmother she had no idea.

★　★　★

Sun was streaming through the open window when Fiona eventually stirred the next morning. She stretched and let the rays warm her face. Her little room always caught the morning light, and even when Doreen offered her a bigger room after Angus died, Fiona didn't want to take her up on it.

Her toes tingled with the stimulation of the stretch and she let out a deep sigh of satisfaction. She looked round at the familiar colour-washed walls and the sprigged curtains flapping gently in the breeze. Rose Cottage always enveloped her in a cocoon of comfort. Here she was safe and happy — and she had so much to be happy about.

Tim had telephoned late last night after Mrs Shaw had left and told Fiona he'd called Ellie and had a long talk with her and put her mind at rest about his safety. He also told her he was returning to work at The Hills today and next weekend he and Alison were going to choose a ring.

Fiona had had a brief word with Alison, who insisted they did a girls' lunch together when she had a free day. Neither of them asked questions about Rory Grainger, and Fiona wondered what story he had strung them after she'd rushed out of the flat. She was sure he would invent something. He was very good at being economical with the truth.

With these thoughts whirring through her brain, Fiona didn't immediately register that someone was knocking on her front door. She glanced at her alarm clock and let out a grunt of surprise. It was ten o'clock. She couldn't remember when she had last slept in so late.

Jumping out of bed she grabbed her dressing gown and, thrusting her arms through the sleeves, ran down the stairs and peered through the spy hole in the door to see who was outside.

Ellie Marsden was on the step, about to have another go at the knocker.

'Hello, dear,' she greeted Fiona as she opened the door. 'Oh, I'm so sorry. Did I wake you?'

'No, I was just getting up,' Fiona replied. 'I slept late. Come in.'

'I could come back if it's not convenient?'

'I'm just about to make some tea. You're very welcome to have a cup.'

'Why don't I make it,' Ellie offered, 'while you get dressed?'

Fiona scampered up the stairs and headed for the shower. She refused to think about what Ellie Marsden was doing on her doorstep until she had showered and found some fresh clothes. After her stay at The Hills she had a mountain of laundry.

She raised her face to the spray of hot water and let it cascade down her body, then she scrubbed hard at her skin with her sponge. She would not think about Rory Grainger. Why did the wretched man keep invading her thoughts when she was trying to get on with her life?

The smell of toast wafted up the stairs as Fiona went back downstairs again. Ellie was already sitting at the kitchen table pouring tea and sorting out butter and marmalade.

'I didn't realise how hungry I was,' she smiled at Fiona, 'until I started making your breakfast. I only had time for a cup of coffee before I rushed out of the house. You do like toast don't you?' she asked anxiously.

'That was lovely of you,' Fiona said, 'Thanks.' She bit into a warm slice liberally coated with orange marmalade. 'Delicious.'

'One of life's great comforts,' Ellie agreed, nibbling on her slice a tad more daintily than Fiona, 'is early morning toast, even if it is served up as elevenses.'

They settled into companionable silence for a few moments while they ate.

'Tim rang me last night and said he'd spoken to you,' Fiona spoke first.

Ellie with a mouth full of toast nodded vigorously at her. After delicately wiping her lips with a piece of kitchen paper, she said, 'I was so pleased to hear from him and we've made things up between us.'

'Good.' Fiona started on a second slice of toast. Now she came to think about it, she couldn't remember when she'd last eaten anything.

'And such news.' Ellie's blue eyes

widened with surprise. 'He tells me he's engaged to that actress, the one who's on television. I like to watch her, but Frank doesn't like the soaps so I can only catch up on them when he's out.'

Swallowing down the impulse to tell Ellie she really ought to assert herself at least when it came to watching television, Fiona said, 'I've met her and she's really lovely, not at all like the character she plays.'

'And you've met Tim too?' Ellie asked carefully.

'I have and it was sibling love at first sight,' Fiona assured her. 'We've got loads of time to make up and as soon as we can we're going to get together again. Tim said something about an engagement party.'

'That would be lovely.' Ellie's face lit up and Fiona could see that as a young woman she would have been very pretty indeed, with her clear blue eyes and once blonde hair — just the sort of girl Angus would have fallen for.

'Actually, it's so wonderful having a

family again.' Fiona poured herself a second cup of tea.

'I am sorry, Fiona,' Ellie said in a quiet voice, 'for what I did. I thought I was acting for the best.'

'You don't need to be sorry,' Fiona replied.

'Can you find it in your heart to forgive me?'

'There's nothing to forgive,' Fiona insisted.

'At times you are so like your mother,' Ellie said. 'She was the sweetest girl in the world. I've got lots of things to show you one day when things have settled down a bit. Perhaps we could even have a nice relaxing spa weekend away together? At The Hills?'

'No!' Fiona snapped. 'Not there.'

Ellie raised an eyebrow. 'As you wish, but it does have a good reputation. That Rory Grainger is a very able manager. Tim loves working with him.'

It was a strain for Fiona to keep smiling at Ellie as she talked about Rory. As soon as she could she managed to change the subject.

'I'm so pleased you contacted me after Doreen died. I was feeling a bit down. The girls at work were sympathetic and so was Mrs Shaw but there was no one I could really talk to.'

'Mrs Shaw said something about you suffering from a broken engagement?'

'George Ross, he married my hairdresser, but I'm over that now,' Fiona insisted, 'and in a way I'm grateful to him. It would have been far worse if we had gone ahead with our wedding and then he'd fallen in love with someone else. As it was, at the time I thought he had broken my heart, but . . . '

'Not any more?' Ellie asked.

'Not any more,' Fiona agreed.

'Good.' Ellie smiled her lovely smile. 'And any time you want to talk to me about anything you'll find that I'm an excellent listener.' She paused then blinked nervously. 'Actually it took me ages to pluck up the courage to write to you and then tell Tim what I'd done, but now I'm so pleased I did.'

'Me too,' Fiona agreed. 'Everything turned out well in the end and I've discovered a whole new family. There's you and Tim, and now Alison's family. She says they're a huge extended family from Essex, I can't wait to meet them.'

'I don't know what Frank will have to say about that,' Ellie began.

'Oh, bother Frank!'

The words were out before Fiona could stop herself. 'I'm sorry, Ellie, but honestly, the way you let him treat you is wrong. It's none of my business but . . .'

'You don't understand,' Ellie restrained her.

'You're right. I don't.'

'You see there's one more thing I haven't told you.'

'I haven't got another brother hidden away somewhere have I?' Fiona's question was a joke but Ellie didn't smile back.

'No. It's nothing like that.' She fiddled with a corner of the kitchen table. 'Did you give your next door neighbour my telephone number?'

'Mrs Shaw? Yes. I hope you don't mind, only she said she wanted to talk to you about something.'

Ellie nodded. 'I met her the once, the night Doreen agreed to look after you. We were sitting in your lounge when she knocked on the door looking for a cup of sugar, or something.'

'That sounds like Mrs Shaw. I'm afraid she's very nosy.'

'She and Doreen were great friends I believe.'

'Mrs Shaw never had any children so she helped to look after me after school when Doreen was working, or away on business with Angus. I owe her a lot.'

'She did the things I should have done,' Ellie said with a sad smile then raising her head, she said, 'I may as well get this over with. If you don't ever want to see me again I'll understand.'

'Ellie,' Fiona's voice rose in concern, 'whatever is it?'

'You see, I hurt Doreen, very badly, and she told your Mrs Shaw about it. It was a stupid, cruel and vicious thing to do.'

'I'm sure it can't have been that bad.'

'I was very much in love with Angus, but I wasn't blind to his faults. He had a roving eye and after I had Gillian, your mother, I wasn't very well. I suppose these days they would call it post-natal depression, but back then, no one really understood that sort of thing.'

'And?' Fiona prompted when Ellie lapsed into silence.

Ellie cleared her throat. 'I can't blame Angus. I wasn't very nice to him. I didn't want him near me. He tried hard to cheer me up, but you know how he liked to be the life and soul of the party and basically I wasn't much fun and not unnaturally he got a bit fed up with me.'

'Are you saying he had an affair?'

'More a casual fling really, I suppose, and it wasn't with Doreen, but when I found out about it I stormed out of the house and went back to live with my parents. I thought Angus would come running after me, but when he didn't I wrote him a silly letter saying I never wanted to see him again.'

'How sad,' Fiona sympathised.

'It was only later I realised he had actually come looking for me but my mother wouldn't let him in the house. She and Angus were always quarrelling. When I found out what she'd done I tried to contact him but then my mother told me she'd heard from a friend of hers that he'd met someone else and that was that. Our marriage was over.'

Ellie did her best to smile but it didn't really work.

'I'm so terribly sorry,' Fiona was able to sympathise quite genuinely.

'Like you, with your George, I got over it in time but I never really forgave my mother. Things were never the same between us afterwards.'

'Sad though it is, Ellie, I can see why your story is so terrible — although it wouldn't raise an eyebrow today.'

'Perhaps not, but there's more. You see I blamed Doreen for coming between Angus and me even though none of it was her fault. She met him long after I'd disappeared from the scene. But Doreen knew that I irrationally held her responsible for what happened.'

'How could she have known that?'

'She swore Mrs Shaw to silence, but I can imagine how she must have felt and the lengths she must have gone through to keep her secret quiet.'

'Her secret?' Fiona was getting more and more confused as she listened to Ellie spinning her tale.

'Angus and I were never divorced.'

'What?'

'I wouldn't agree to it. It was the only hold I had over him and I didn't want to give it up. I knew my being married to Angus annoyed my mother too but I couldn't help myself.'

Ellie bit her lip and waited for Fiona's reaction.

'So you're telling me Doreen and

Angus weren't married?' Fiona repeated slowly, trying to get her head around the shock of it all.

'No — I mean yes, I'm telling you they were never husband and wife.'

'But what about you and Frank?'

'I treated him rather badly, I'm afraid. You see he felt about me the same way I felt about Angus. He loved me and was prepared to wait. We only got married after Angus died. I was officially Angus's widow so that's how I knew he had died. Of course I wrote a letter of sympathy to Doreen but she never replied, and after that all contact between us ceased.'

Fiona blinked at Ellie, unable to speak.

'Mrs Shaw knew because Doreen told her in case she no longer wanted to be friends with a woman who was living with someone else's husband.'

Fiona's lips twisted in a wry smile. 'Mrs Shaw has her faults, but a lack of loyalty isn't one of them. I don't suppose it would have made an atom of difference to their relationship.'

'Mrs Shaw assured me it didn't, but you read my letter out to her?'

'Yes.'

'I gather also that Tim came visiting, looking for you?'

'Yes, while I was at The Hills.'

'Mm, well, all this seems to have galvanised Mrs Shaw into action and she thought if I was about to take my rightful place in your life as your grandmother, then it was my place to tell you what I'd done. By the way, she doesn't mince her words does she?'

'Er . . . no . . . ' Fiona conceded with a smile, imagining Mrs Shaw really going to town on poor Ellie.

'She was perfectly right of course,' Ellie agreed, 'and now I have told you everything I'll go. I'll understand if you don't ever want to see me again, but all I can say is I'm so very sorry, Fiona. Love makes you do funny things and sometimes we only realise what a big mistake we've made until after it's too late to put it right.'

'No.' Fiona put out a hand to detain Ellie. 'Don't go. I can't say all this hasn't been the most huge shock, but it doesn't alter the love I felt for Doreen. She never told me any of it, but I know she loved me and she gave me the most wonderful childhood. She wouldn't have done that if you hadn't made the supreme sacrifice of giving me up.'

Tears were now trickling freely down Ellie's cheeks. 'Frank and I would have taken you, Fiona, but you see we weren't married either. Frank thought if we were responsible for Tim and he stayed at boarding school in this country while we were abroad, the authorities wouldn't object and everything would be all right. By the time we were married Doreen and I had lost touch.'

'I see.' Fiona didn't know what else to say.

'It's like something out of a Greek tragedy isn't it?' Ellie said. 'By today's standards it all sounds so terribly tame, but things were different back then.'

'Have you told Tim all this?'

'It was too late to speak to him last night after Mrs Shaw contacted me so I phoned him this morning at work. As he didn't know Doreen it wasn't so much of a shock to him.'

'Do you fancy a glass of wine?' Fiona asked on impulse.

'At this time of the day? It's barely lunch time.' Ellie looked shocked.

'Why not? Why don't we drink to the start of our new life together? Tell you what, I'll ask Mrs Shaw to join us.' There was a fleeting look of panic in Ellie's eyes. 'You've got to meet her again some time Ellie, and she's probably hovering in her garden now, if she'll have seen your car parked outside.'

'Frank . . . '

'Isn't here and if you don't tell him I won't either.'

After a moment's hesitation Ellie broke into a huge smile. 'Why not? Go for it, Fiona,' she urged. 'By the way,' she said, as her granddaughter stood up.

'Yes?'

'A word of advice from me. If you ever fall in love again, please don't let foolish pride ruin things.'

* * *

'Goodness me, would you look at that?'

Mrs Shaw roared with laughter at the sight of Ellie Marsden trying to tango with Alison's father.

'I must say her family know how to party,' Fiona laughed.

The ballroom was bulging at the seams with partygoers, all intent on having a good time. The huge double windows were opened out onto the gardens, which were strewn with fairy lights and summer candles in jars. The spray from the water garden kept the atmosphere cool and several couples had taken the opportunity to stroll in the grounds and enjoy the late night air.

'Isn't she a lovely girl?' Mrs Shaw smiled at Alison as she chatted to Jim Shaw. 'Knows how to put people at their ease doesn't she? And isn't Tim a handsome boy? They make a lovely couple. I knew Tim was your brother,' Mrs Shaw confided, 'at least I suspected it, that day he came calling at the cottage. You know, I never thought I'd hear myself say this, Fiona, but I quite like Ellie Marsden. She's not half as stuck up as she seems to be when you get to know her properly, is she?'

The coffee party that had turned into an early drinks party at Rose Cottage had certainly broken the ice between the two women, who were fast on the verge of becoming firm friends.

'Isn't that man waving at you, dear?' Mrs Shaw pointed across the room.

'No, I don't think so.'

'Yes he is,' Mrs Shaw insisted. 'You go and network. Don't worry about me. I might have another go at the buffet in a minute when Jim's finished chatting up that young lady of Tim's.'

'No really, I . . . I'm perfectly happy where I am . . . ' Fiona began to protest.

'Off you go,' Mrs Shaw said firmly and turned her back pointedly and started talking to an aunt of Alison's.

Fiona got reluctantly to her feet.

'Hello, Rory,' she said as he walked towards her.

'You are speaking to me then?' He quirked an eyebrow at her, a hesitant smile on his lips.

'Where's Issy?' she asked pointedly.

'Last I heard she was sunning herself in the south of France on a yacht with the latest man in her life.'

Fiona was annoyed to discover she was blushing with pleasure at seeing him again. He was dressed in a tight white shirt, ruffled and open at the neck and it gave him the appearance of a modern-day Cavalier. She had chosen her own aquamarine dress with care and tried to convince herself it was in Tim and Alison's honour.

She cleared her throat. 'Thank you for agreeing to have Alison's engagement party here,' she said.

'Here is the only place Alison could

think of where we physically eject unwanted journalists.'

'And those you even vaguely suspect of working for the newspapers?'

'Are you ever going to let me forget that?'

'Probably not,' Fiona said.

'Would you like to dance?' he asked.

'I don't do the tango.' Fiona glanced across to where Ellie had finished her performance and was staggering towards the seat Fiona had just vacated beside Mrs Shaw.

'Neither do I,' Rory said with a feigned look of horror. 'My back would never stand it. Come on, this one's a waltz. I can just about manage that.'

On the dance floor he slid his arm around Fiona's waist and drew her body firmly towards his.

'Sorry, did I tread on your toes?' he asked. Fiona shook her head. She wasn't thinking very clearly. Ellie's words were echoing around her head. *Don't let pride ruin your life.*

Was she being silly because she and

Rory had started off on the wrong foot? He had apologised for their initial misunderstanding and Tim had told Fiona Issy had been banned from The Hills. Fiona didn't want to repeat Ellie's mistakes, mistakes she suspected Ellie still regretted to this day.

Despite his comments, Rory proved to be a very good dancer. He was light on his feet and he led Fiona around the floor, expertly steering her away from the less competent members of Alison's family who were trying to have a go at proper dancing. Elbows were flying in all directions and they weren't too fussy where they put their feet.

'Sorry.' Fiona ducked under an arm that threatened to hit her in the face.

Her head landed on Rory's shoulder and as she clung onto him for support she caught a glance of Alison making encouraging gestures with her hands at the sight of the two of them dancing together. Tim was standing by her side, a proud smile on his face.

'Are you all right?' Rory asked,

steering Fiona away from the mayhem on the dance floor. His lips felt warm against her hair.

'Yes.' Her voice resembled a froggy croak.

This was the first time she had been this close to Rory Grainger and it was a heady experience. She could feel the beat of his heart against hers.

Dancing with her ex-fiancé, George, had always been a trial. He would mangle her feet then complain that she wasn't following the beat. With Rory things were so different. The floor felt soft under her feet as he twirled her around in perfect time to the music.

'Do you think we could start again, now that everything's out in the open?' He murmured in her ear. 'I mean I know you don't like red-headed men, but . . . '

Fiona raised her eyes. His face was so close to hers the stubble on his chin scratched her cheek.

'Tim's got sandy hair,' she said, 'and I like him.'

'Let's leave Tim out of this,' Rory insisted in a low, husky voice. 'We're talking about you and me.'

'There is no you and me,' Fiona insisted.

'I'm not very good at playing games, Fiona. You ran out on me once at Alison's flat. If you run out on me again I won't come running after you.'

His words struck a chilling reminder of the way Ellie had behaved after she suspected Angus of having an affair. 'If we're going to start again, you've got to re-think your ideas on how you talk to me.'

Ellie's experience or not, Fiona was not going to let Rory treat her the way Frank treated Ellie.

'What do you mean?' he demanded.

'For a start, I won't be bossed around and I'll not play the little woman.'

'Fine with me,' Rory said a hint of a smile curving the corners of his eyes. 'Any other orders?'

'I don't like having my word questioned.'

'Neither do I. I told you, Issy . . . '

'And I don't want to talk about your ex-girlfriend either.'

'Still arguing?' Alison drifted by on Tim's arm.

She looked stunning in ivory silk. A solitaire diamond sparkled on the third finger of her left hand as it rested on Tim's shoulder. With a saucy wink at Fiona she steered Tim towards the more vigorous of the dancers. 'Better go and rescue my aunt,' she said, 'before she does someone a physical injury.'

'Fiona?' Rory spoke slowly.

'Yes?'

'Why don't we stop talking and finish this waltz? Then how about I take you into the garden afterwards?'

'Why?' she demanded.

'Because,' he moved his lips back towards her hair again, 'there are far too many people around at the moment and I'd rather like to kiss you and I'd prefer to do it in private.'

'That sounds like a very good idea,' Fiona raised her head, 'except for one thing,' she said with a slow smile.

'What now,' Rory raised his eyebrows in exasperation, 'more objections?'

'Just the one.'

'And that is?'

'I don't think I can wait until the end of the waltz.'

THE END

We do hope that you have enjoyed reading this large print book.

Did you know that all of our titles are available for purchase?

We publish a wide range of high quality large print books including:
Romances, Mysteries, Classics
General Fiction
Non Fiction and Westerns

Special interest titles available in large print are:
The Little Oxford Dictionary
Music Book, Song Book
Hymn Book, Service Book

Also available from us courtesy of Oxford University Press:
Young Readers' Dictionary
(large print edition)
Young Readers' Thesaurus
(large print edition)

For further information or a free brochure, please contact us at:
Ulverscroft Large Print Books Ltd.,
The Green, Bradgate Road, Anstey,
Leicester, LE7 7FU, England.
Tel: (00 44) **0116 236 4325**
Fax: (00 44) **0116 234 0205**

Other titles in the
Linford Romance Library:

RACHEL'S COMING HOME

Gillian Villiers

When her parents run into difficulties running their boarding kennels, Rachel Collington decides to resign from her job and return home to help out. The first customer she encounters is arrogant Philip Milligan, who is nowhere near as friendly as his two collies. Gradually though, he begins to thaw — but just as Rachel is wondering if she has misjudged him, it seems that someone is intent on sabotaging the kennels' reputation.

HEALING LOVE

Cara Cooper

Dr James Frayne's personal life is in meltdown and it is beginning to affect his work. Becky, his Practice Manager, is deeply concerned and wants to help. But Dr James cannot afford to let her in on his secret — if she discovers what's troubling him, it could lose him his job. When his cold efficiency and her powers of deduction collide, sparks fly and emotions are stirred — changing both their lives forever . . .